THE BLACK GARDEN

edited by Christopher Allan Death

CHRIS FREND JUY
2008

CORPULENT INSANITY PRESS

Fort Collins, Colorado

Text set in Times New Roman.
Title text set in Haettenschweiler.
Other text set in Incantation and Ghastly Panic.

ISBN-13: 978-0-578-00798-4

Cover art by Inzekkt
Interior art by Chris Friend
Back cover art by Steve Cartwright

Praise for *The Black Garden*:

"*The Black Garden*, edited by Christopher Allan Death, is a darkly sinister collection of short stories that will surely help cultivate your black thumb! Filled with eight eerie and terrifying tales, *The Black Garden* will find a way to crawl under your skin with its creeping tendrils of terror!"
   -Fatally-Yours.com

"*The Black Garden* is a roller coaster of horror. One moment you're walking on a tropical island, the next spiders are crawling out your eyeballs. A lot of fun, but definitely not for the squeamish."
   -K.T. Pinto, author of *The Books of Insanity*

"Rumors of horror's death have been greatly exaggerated. The genre is alive and kicking within the dark pages of *The Black Garden* — an anthology of creepy, hair-raising stories by new, up-and-coming authors. Read it. Get excited about horror again."
   -Fred Wiehe, author of *Strange Days* and a member of the Horror Writers Association

"Evil grows — literally and metaphorically — throughout this *Black Garden*, an anthology by up-and-comers whose stories tend to call to mind EC Comics in all the best ways. Short, nasty and pointed, like exotic thorns, some of these tales may well stick with you … and take root."
   -W.D. Gagliani, author of *Wolf's Trap* and *Wolf's Gambit*

"*The Black Garden* is hybrid horror anthology; fertile in both powerful bizarro head-melters and cool conventional chillers. This collection of eight stories will plant small seeds of unease that niggle as they grow into creeping tendrils of horror. Visit Peterson's Moreau-esque freak show. Let Anderson give you another great reason to avoid weeding. Take a peek at Dunwoody's unsettling Swift-like world. You want something mythical and trippy? Lee's got you covered. And White has a creature feature that packs a punch for you. Polson gets a little classic King on the go and Dickson adds that Koontz flavour. And to round it off? What better than Dowker's gruesome, unflinching body-shocker?

Pay heed. You're going to want a weed-whacker in your hands before traipsing into this garden. Thorns, needled flytrap teeth, creepy crawlies. That's the kids' stuff. Turn over a couple of stones. See what happens."
   -Gerard Brennan, author of *Posession, Obsession and a Diesel Compression Engine*

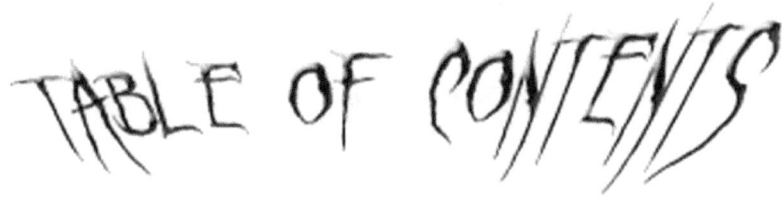

To Feed the Little Children
by Sharon M. White

"Lydia began reaching for the diner's grimy door when a large, warm hand squeezed her shoulder. Fighting back a grin, she allowed her muscles to sag, imitating submission to a stronger force. The man's pleasure at this was evident, the way the tangy, acrid aroma grew thicker around him."

Care and Feeding of the Old Flat Mile
by Aaron A. Polson

"Three figures shimmered in the moonlight. They appeared to be teenage boys, somewhere between sixteen and nineteen, but they all seemed strange. Their faces were pinched together, too gaunt and pale, even in the moonlight. Maggie tried to muster a friendly smile, and the boys' lips cracked open in response."

Aria
by Allison M. Dickson

"The country landscape, blanketed in shadows, rushed by as the black Lexus picked up more and more speed. The needle of the speedometer was edging into three-digit territory when Mark gave up pleading and resorted to screaming."

Ill Conceived
by Felicity Dowker

"She sat motionless on the toilet, feeling shocked. She'd just had her fingers inside herself for the first time in...she couldn't remember how long. The fleshy heat had been foreign and overwhelming, and she looked down in wonder at her fingers, daubed with blood."

Author Bios

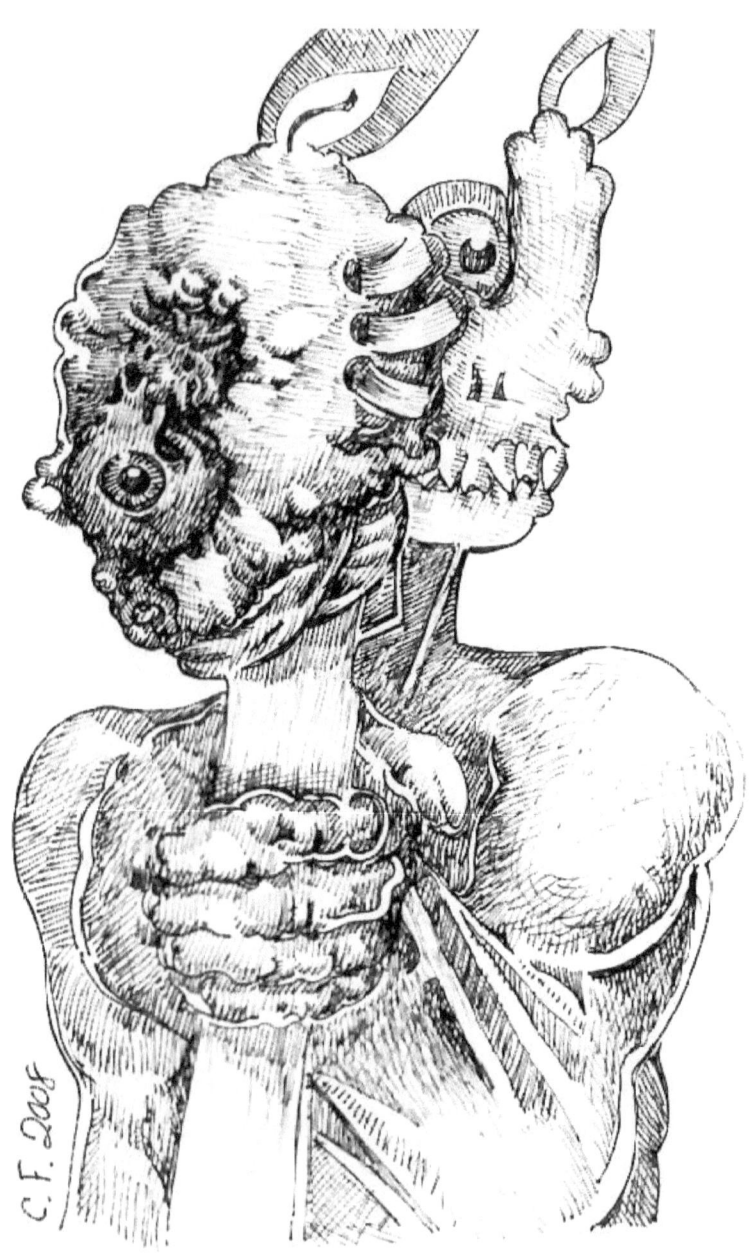

THE KENNEL

by Evan J. Peterson

The Kennel is both a laboratory and a playhouse. Come in and see, if you have a strong stomach. This is the theater in which performers are conscripted. Each one is an involuntary clown, some with new grins in unlikely places.

Consider me the ultimate showman: an impresario, a barker, a director, and an animal trainer. I create glee from pathetic buffoons and geeks to make gawkers feel better about themselves. It's my calling, to twist the recognizable and satirize the natural order. I mock God, and my parodies are perfect in the severity of their flaws.

Levity is the highest public service, you know. I consider myself the prime minister of relief. I traffic in entertainment– the abjection of others on whom fortune has defecated. Still, this is just a means to an elegant end. Let's be honest, it's about the work. The bonecraft, the tugging of meat and fur into new shapes– I'd do it for free, but if a senator with disposable cash and a hard-on for bioengineering will pay through the nose (a fascinating organ) for domesticated misfortune, how can I refuse?

The Kennel also functions as a respite from outside life. The more time I spend in here, the less I spend out there. Food is delivered. I have everything I need. I like to sleep in here, listening to my creations' bodies expanding and contracting with breath. I'm comforted by the idea that we all inhale one another's exhalations. It's safer in here, even with the suffering.

Just look at what's become of the world. The Anonymity Act has outlawed celebrities, and now every political party is endorsed by ill-conceived cartoon characters and invisible musicians. Assassinations have their own channel and have become a form of staged reality. People are soothed by the predictable. I try to inject a bit of randomness into a society dying of stagnation. Nothing is dangerous anymore, but everything is lethal.

Come, I'll take you on the nickel tour. The vats are over here. The copper feels nice. Touch it. The nubby bolts are like metal nipples. Each vat is a cauldron of plasma, amniotic and primordial. Some are mere soup stock. Others, such as this one, contain little friends in the process of gestation. Prenatal vitamins are dripped or pumped in via these pipes and tubes. The embryonic experiments have a special place in my heart, each one congealing as though it were my own molten cyst.

Next to the vats are the tanks. Some require aeration, others are self-contained ecosystems. So delicate. Did you know I'm a Pisces? I think that's why I relate to the swimmers and the floaters. They aren't all aquatic, either. Herman the merman here can't survive outside of-ten gallons of human urine. He's neither *mer* nor *man*, but more of an axolotl.

Over here is the chemical station. I have all the usual glucose and strychnine, embalming fluid and semen, plus a variety of pharmaceuticals: tranquilizers, atavistic stimulants, steroids, endocrine suppositories, anesthetics for wimpier subjects, thalidomide. I even have a microscope of my own invention, crude though it is. It has a bifocal lens that can see into the future simultaneously with the present. That way, I know the results of experiments as I'm performing them. Quite the time saver, though it does take a bit of the fun out of watching a human ear bloom gradually from a fungal culture.

Petri dishes are kept in locked storage while their contents evolve. They interfere with one another from time to time, either through biological contamination or brutal force. Occasionally, that results in serendipity, much like the discovery of penicillin. Unfortunately, it more often corrupts whole samples, and I'm forced

14

to destroy them before they can do any more damage. Wouldn't want those escaping, would we?

This door leads to an alcove wherein I conduct experiments in metaphysics and parapsychology. I can't show you that room.

We'll view the cages in a moment, but first, the gurney. Surgery is an art, you know, and I'm a fan of mixed media. Tinkering under the microscope is a fashionable, fitting place to start, but to really torture a masterpiece out of phenotype, you've got to tie it to the table. My instruments may look crude compared to, say, laser scalpels, but when those devices malfunction they can turn a penis into a burnt spaghetti strand. I have some precious phalli around here that I'd rather not risk. I smith my own tools, thank you very much, and I've seen no glitches yet. My mother always said, "You must create new instruments for new demands. There will always be new fetishes for new bodies."

There are so many new bodies incarnating around here. It's a carnival of birth. Just the right mix of chaos and design. It's a meeting of opposites in prolific clash. In many ways, I serve the very Creator I mock. Each new flower of flesh is a permutation of beauty, elegant in asymmetry, precious in pathology. I fill each phylum with original sins. Isn't that what the Demiurge would want – a bowing chorus of chimerical singers, all raising their squealing voices in rasps of praise?

They like to vie for the spotlight, too. The acoustics in the lab are superb. If I flip the operating table around, it becomes a platform. Want to see some of them tap dance?

Subject Y-1745: I was reading a collection of folk tales of extinct indigenous peoples when I came up with the idea for this one. It looks spidery, but there's no arachnid material there. I've married the ghost crab to the frilled lizard and wrapped them around a thylacine. It makes a god--awful clicky-hissing sound through those mandibles, but some folks seem to like it. The throat fringe reminds most people of a noble ruff. I like the name "Basilisk" for these, but the customers affectionately call them "Queen Elizabeths."

These must stay caged. An American noise band, The Shattered Fixtures, bought two for their next record. They planned to record the Basilisks' unique mating calls. Unfortunately, the Basilisks got loose in the studio and stripped the percussionist's legs to the bone in forty five seconds.

Many of my little friends are inspired by world mythology. Most people don't realize that extinction only adds to the romance of a culture. No nostalgia without loss. Alive, they're a bothersome collection of savages. It's not until they're all dead that their relics attain full value.

Subject R-33: I've recently taken to calling her Matilda. She's a limp thing, ragged, an inarticulate doll. My current favorite. Getting the limbs to spool like that took commitment. Now, notice the seemingly impossible depth of the eye pits, and the flatness of her head. You should be able to see the inside back of the skull, or even something cerebral, but no. Just darkness – fresh, clean, open air. She breathes through there, you know.

Matilda is a delicate balance of bone and cartilage. To achieve the full aesthetic effect, she must slump like a brokeback, but retain the ability to shuffle around. Ironically, she may be the most humanoid project in the laboratory, but don't let that fool you. Not a shred of human DNA in her. Lemur, yes. Devil ray and brittlestar. Looks like a real girl, doesn't she? Slap a little *Maybelline* on anything, and it'll look like a face after a while.

Subject J-2889: This one requires no food to live. I've teased his chemistry to the pinnacle of efficiency. He survives solely on fresh air and his own solid waste, which is fit for human consumption. It tastes like sulfurous honey, or a sweet and spicy egg. Of all the current residents, this fellow has been with me the longest. I feel rather attached to him, probably because he embodies roughly 12% of my own genetic coding. Soon, I may let him out of his pen. He's quite docile.

Care to pet him? He has no teeth to bite, no claws to rend. I'm particularly proud of finally getting the feathers to blend in with the fur. If you startle him, the feathers stand out like-spines. But don't worry – they couldn't prick the surface of a puddle.

I'm not sure what went so right with him. I find his noisome diet to be deliciously despicable, but the buyers want something less cuddly. No one will purchase him, and I can't give him away. The art of grotesquery is often a thankless discipline.

Subject A-5609: Needs more time to marinade, but a possible hole-in-one. It's not just funny to point at, either. It's a pleasure module. The muscular tentacles are strong enough for power games, but not enough to pose a real threat. The exterior is all mucous membranes, like the inside of an eyelid.

Look here. This is possibly my most brilliant breakthrough in carnal ergonomics. Namely, the straps and buckles. It grows its own restraints. Thank you, that's very flattering, but it wasn't so difficult. Just a matter of guiding the chiton, the mother of pearl, into the right morphology for a clasp. The straps are undifferentiated tissue.

This creation is utterly wearable, and quite comfortable if you ask me.

Subject D-8942: Take a greyhound genome. Turn off the chromosomal toggles that tell it to develop front legs. Stimulate the ass-end markers to work overtime. What comes out of the vat is a puppy with only hind limbs but two thick, heavy tails. For the first three months, it will propel itself forward, dragging its face along the ground like a plow. Then, as it learns to adapt, it will stand upright. This form of locomotion causes it to seesaw as it moves in a delicate balance between torso and tails. It looks a bit like a kangaroo when it really gets going around the house, but it can't punch you.

Subject Q-0003: I'm not ready to talk about him yet.

Subjects H-88: I felt rather whimsical, so I decided to work with conjoined human twins. Initially, I code-named this brood "the Jack and Jill iterations." My goal, still unrealized, was to design hermaphroditic twins, then refine them so they looked as though one was male and one female. That would've been the ultimate coupling: identical and fraternal, one flesh as brother and sister, husband and wife. I've since abandoned such lofty aspirations.

These subjects still appear monozygotic. Joined at the head, I've fused the one's jaws to—the other's skull, so one is constantly chewing at the other's head like Ugolino and Ruggieri. The selective melding is a painstaking process, both for them and for me. It requires gently nudging the embryo in just the right way, snipping it here, binding it there, and so on. The concentration required is agonizing.

I've sold many others from this batch. The chief of the Morality Guard was awe-struck by the pair that simultaneously sodomize one

17

another. He asked me, "Are they *people*?" I assured him that their brains were genetically reduced to the size of a squirrel's, that their skulls contained mostly water. "Not people in the sense that you and I are," I told him. He thought about that for a long moment before pulling out his wallet.

So, who would you like to take home today? What about Matilda? You look like a doll collector to me. You could put her in a tutu like a baboon ballerina and teach her to piqué. Wouldn't that be a hit at dinner parties?

Don't pretend that you're only here to turn your nose up and clutch your throat. You came to the Kennel to get an eyeful. You're already an accomplice, a witness. Evolution is cruel. Art is unmerciful. Do remember, I'm under the protection of the Morality Guard. As far as they're concerned, what goes on in here is my business.

I leave you with two options. Stay a few more minutes and make a purchase, or stay until I've exhausted the limits of your flesh. You, too, are a beautiful animal.

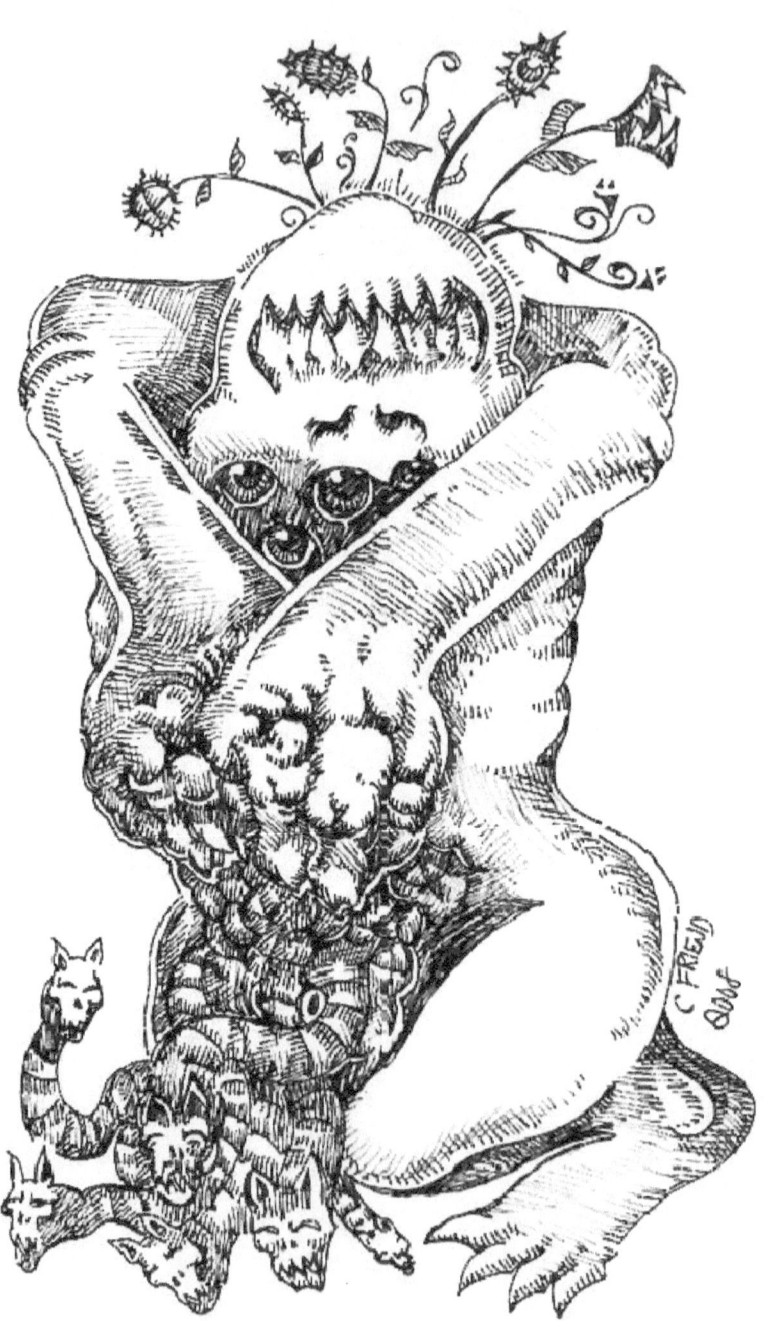

THE INDIGENOUS FLORA AND FAUNA OF A SMALL TROPICAL ISLAND

by Sam W. Anderson

Mervin had just finished slathering the SPF 50 on his reachable areas when the cabin door burst open.

"Perv!" Soda Pop shouted. Adorned in a Hawaiian shirt, Bermuda shorts and sunglasses that cost more than Mervin's car, Soda stood in the doorway with two Red Stripe beers in hand and a goofy smile plastered on his face. "Come here and give your old buddy a big man-hug."

"How's about giving a guy a beer before you feel him up, eh?" The two men erupted in laughter and embraced with a familiarity that erased lost years. Mervin realized how much he'd missed his college chums – even the trust-fund blessed Joseph "Soda-Pop" McStain. "How you been, Soda? What are you doing now?"

"Same ol' same old, you know. Worked with Dad for a while, but that was borderline disastrous. So, now I just hang out. Dirty work, but I manage okay." Soda handed Mervin a key-chain bottle opener. Mervin noted the Mercedes key as he popped the beer's cap free. "It's good to see you, Perv. Could've brought your hair along, though."

Mervin rubbed his bare pate. "Let's just say my hair and I have parted not-so-amicably."

The two men sipped their beers, smiles glowing. Mervin evaluated his former roommate, wondering how Soda hadn't aged in ten years. He still sported the same perma-tan and mop of sandy hair that he'd been blessed with back in college.

"Anybody else here, yet?" Mervin asked before their brief silence grew uncomfortable.

"Not yet. Joey and Zack are sailing out in the morning. Haven't heard from Biggie for a couple of months. He knocked up his old lady and was kind of waffling – like that's an excuse to miss this."

"Biggie's coming – sent me an email Tuesday saying he'll be here tomorrow." Mervin drank from the stubby bottle and released a joyously juvenile belch. "I was getting ready to look around. Want to come with?"

"For a bit. I haven't been here since freshman year, you know. I think Dad completely forgot he owns this." Soda drained the rest of his beer in a large gulp. He, too, belched in such a loud tone that it echoed inside the cabin. "But I want to get back and catch some 'Z's.' I don't think there's going to be much sleeping over the next few days." Soda Pop raised his empty bottle and Mervin clinked his against it.

"Not if we do this right." Both men found this funnier than it truly was, and Mervin realized he couldn't erase the grin from his face. "As you so eloquently put it back in college: 'We can sleep when we're dead.'"

"You said it, Merv the Perv."

They walked along the flagstone pathway connecting the six one-room bungalows facing the beach. Palm fronds and blossom-engorged flame trees sprouted between the cabins, highlighting the lilies and orchards lining the pathway with bright colors. Omnipresent, the calming surf tickled the beach and Mervin smelled the fresh scent of salty air. Grass-thatched roofs topped each cabin, completing the tropical ambiance.

"Still got that lawn-mowing business, then?" Soda asked, opening a fresh Red Stripe.

"It's landscape construction, moron."

"Whatever."

"I still have it, but barely. One of my dumb-ass laborers lost control of the Bobcat last summer and went through the back of a two-million dollar house." Mervin shook his head, still unable to believe the story he was repeating. "Both my guy and the homeowner are suing, and it ain't looking good."

"Ouch, Dude," Soda said. "That sucks royal ass."

"Yeah, ouch – that's what my wallet said." Mervin released an uncomfortable chuckle.

Twenty minutes passed. The pair found themselves back in front of Mervin's cabin. The moderate early morning was giving way to the usual tropical heat. Mervin felt the flagstones warming through his three-dollar flip flops. Studying the walkway, he imagined the path as a focal point in one of his landscape designs.

"For a deserted island, this place sure is well maintained," Mervin said.

"I noticed that, too. When I brought out the generators and shit last week, I thought I'd have some cleaning up to do, but it was almost perfect." Soda belched again. "I'm not bitching, you know. Just meant less work for me."

"Like you'd know what work was."

"Fuck you, Perv."

Mervin pointed to the flagstone path. "Looks like you could have done something with that, though." Through one of the joints, a flowering weed grew. It stood just short of eight-inches high and sported tri-petaled, cyanic blossoms.

"Leave it be," Soda Pop said. "I know it's not your nature, but you're on vacation. No landscaping, you know."

"You're right." Mervin crouched down, inspecting the angry-looking specimen. "But since I'm on vacation, I'm not going to let this damn thing grow here and bother me all weekend."

He reached for the base of the weed, trying to avoid its thorns. He clamped down on the stalk. It felt meatier than he expected. A small electric charge surged up his arm, and he felt a thorn pierce his thumb.

"Hey-Zeus, Mother of Christ!"

"Is the little weedie-poo getting the best of you, Perv?" Soda shook his head, guffawing.

Mervin answered with an eardrum-piercing scream. He bit down on his lip with enough force to draw blood. A seizure crippled him and drool trickled down his chin. He tried pulling his hand free, but the weed clamped down on it. He dropped to his knees, the crunching blow hollow against the flagstone.

"Perv! What is it?" Soda dropped his beer and ran behind Mervin. Mervin felt his friend's arms reach around his chest. The men pulled, but the weed tightened its grip on Mervin's thumb. He screamed again.

"On three," Soda said. He counted down and both men shrieked with effort on three. The weed snapped audibly. Mervin and Soda fell to the sun-heated pathway like winners of an unfair tug-of-war.

Mervin held his hand to his chest, blood staining his white tank top. "Holy shit! That fucking thing bit me."

He felt his companion's gaze. Soda leered at him. "You playing me, Perv?"

"Dude, I'm bleeding here." He held up his thumb. A good-sized chunk of flesh was missing. "Does this look like I'm playin'?"

Both men turned to the broken weed. Now crimson-covered, it held onto the missing bit of Mervin's thumb."

"Jesus. Perv, how's about you don't touch anything the rest of the weekend, k?"

Mervin attempted a laugh, but mustered only a snorting hiccup. His face twisted in pain. His eyes watered and the blood rushed from his head.

"This is really starting to burn, man." He slipped off his tank top and wrapped his thumb. The shirt filled with blood faster than he'd expected.

"Are you okay? I can sail back to the mainland…"

"Fuck that! I've waited all winter for this trip. I can handle a little pinprick from a weed. Just give me some time." A tear formed and stuck on the stubble of his cheek. He forced a painful excuse for a smile. "Besides, I'll probably drink enough to kill any infection anyway."

"You sure? You look like you're hurting, you know." Soda stood up and brushed the sand from his shorts and hairless legs.

"Yeah, I'm cool. Hurts like a son-of-a-bitch, but I'm a big boy."

"If you want, I got something for the pain."

Mervin laughed. "You ain't changed one bit, have you?"

"Hold on. Dr. Soda will fix you up." Soda jogged up the path and disappeared into his cabin. A few minutes later, he emerged with a plastic baggie in one hand and a first-aid kit in the other. He set down the kit and opened up the baggie filled with an assortment of pills. "The pharmacy is now open."

"I don't know, man." Mervin struggled to his feet, holding the t-shirt. "I remember some of your pharmaceutical experiments when we lived in the house on Laurel Street."

"You ever going to forgive me for that?"

"Hell no."

Soda removed three large pills. "You should get on with your life, Perv. Forgiveness is divine, or some bullshit like that, you know." He swallowed one of the pills dry and extended his hand to give Mervin the remaining two.

"Hey, ass-licker, you put a hit of acid in my coffee. I had a botany midterm that morning."

"True. But what did you get on that test?"

Mervin shrugged, unable to maintain his air of indignity. "I think an 'A,' actually."

"Then shut the fuck up and get over it."

Soda nudged his friend with the hand containing the pills. "Take these if you need them later. Now, give me your hand we'll get that boo-boo bandaged up."

Mervin accepted the pills and slid them into his shorts pocket. He presented the damaged hand.

"Jesus, man," Soda said. "I see some bone here. That weed totally kicked your ass, you know."

"Want to feel what that's like?"

Soda exploded with laughter. "I think you better grow some, Perv, before you go spouting off like that. Things may have changed since college, but not that much."

Mervin grimaced as Soda wrapped his thumb. The finished job looked like something a five-year old could have done, but Mervin thought the hand might be feeling better now that it was protected from the tropical air. Dark red filled the gauze.

"Watch yourself, now. I don't want some petunia eating your leg or something," Soda said. "Take the first-aid kit, in case you need to clean the bandage, you know. I'm off to enjoy that pill and take a nap."

Mervin watched Soda disappear into the cabin two doors down. Once the door shut, he looked to the ocean and saw Soda's sailboat moored by the lone dock. Mervin had paid 200 pesos to some Mexican fisherman for a ride to the island. His supplies consisted of a knapsack of clothes and a cooler of low-budget beer, the same brand he'd drank since college. He removed the pills from his pocket.

"Thanks, Soda," he said. "And fuck you, too." He forced the pills down in a ravenous manner. His hand throbbed in tune with his accelerated heartbeat. Entering his bungalow, he collapsed on the feather bed.

* * *

Paralysis seized him. Just his eyes could move, and they viewed his surroundings only in shades of gray. He guessed, based upon his perspective, that he laid prone on the ground outside the bungalow. The oppressive, humid heat weighed on him.

Focusing on the cabin's front window, a feverish rage pulsed through his system. He knew not at what he directed his anger, but it consumed him. Bile-like, he tasted it in the back of the mouth which he could not feel. He wanted to kill something. Anything. The thought frightened and excited him simultaneously, as if his mind worked on two different planes. His world consisted of the cabin before him, and this intense hatred.

He felt famished. Not so much a pit-of-the-stomach type of hunger, but rather every cell within him craved nourishment. He had no awareness of his body, yet his instincts screamed for sustenance. His mind focused on his basest desires while unable to form a clear thought.

Stuck in one position, the shadows morphed as the sun progressed throughout the morning. The heat intensified. The rage simmered. His hunger swelled.

At last, he sensed movement. His synapses exploded with activity as a shadow crept into view. He commanded himself to attack, but his body refused the order. His rage and hunger fused. Attempting a scream, nothing sounded.

A scorpion scurried into view. The vibration of minute footfalls shook the flagstone and 'heard' it approach without truly hearing anything. The arachnid stopped on the pathway, sunning itself. Curling its tail, it flaunted its threatening stinger. Scuttling closer, the scorpion reared up on its back four legs.

Pangs. He felt actual pangs of hunger; pangs of hate; pangs of frustration. A meal sat mere inches away, but it may as well have been miles. If he could, he would have cried.

As the scorpion turned away, leaving him behind to starve, something shot forward. The action occurred with such speed, he didn't see what had happened. The prey had disappeared from his sight. He sensed the exoskeleton crushing; he thought he should have heard it. The warmth of nourishment filled him for a brief respite, invigorating his body, but only enough to tease his appetite.

Again, the shadows changed. He became stronger, sturdier, as time progressed. He waited for something else to move into striking range, but sensed no vibrations. A sense of urgency pulsed through him, as if something must be done or a chance would be forever lost.

He barely recognized the man. Soda crouched before him, removing a pair of expensive shades. Soda's expression changed - from curiosity to horror.

* * *

The throbbing in his right hand jolted Mervin awake. Grogginess from the pill blanketed his mind, and a meddlesome itch gnawed at his thumb. Bolts of pain shot up his arm like something had burrowed into the exposed bone, feeding on the surrounding skin of the damaged thumb. Violet-tinted blood soaked the bandage, coagulating to form a crude cast. Green fuzz sprouted along the gauze's edges. Mervin thought the blood had cemented the bandage to the bed. He tried pulling free, but failed. The harder he pulled, the more pain he suffered.

"Soda!" he yelled in a phlegm-choked call.

He tugged at the tape around the bandage. A flash of pain caused another scream. He wiped away the tears, focusing on his hand. The skin around the bandage had turned bluish and scaly. Upon closer inspection, the bandage's fuzz appeared more like tiny leaves budding.

"You gotta' be fucking kidding me. Pain pills my ass." He rubbed his eyes again and refocused his vision. He definitely saw leaves. "Soda, you cocksucker!"

He pulled with all his strength, gritting his teeth as the agony intensified. His hand separated from the sheet enough for him to see the roots that had burrowed into the mattress. Using his free hand, he reached to touch the roots.

A shoot slithered through a crease in the gauze. The pale, thin shoot rapidly thickened into a tendril approximately a foot long. Mervin's hand burned as if the sprout were a rope being pulled through a hole in his thumb. Leaves budded and unfolded, exposing their menacing thorns. The sickly, off-white color transformed into a dark emerald as Mervin watched in horror.

27

The door banged against the bungalow wall and Soda rushed through the opening.

"Dude! You need to see what's goin…" Soda stopped at the foot of the bed. The beer bottle slipped from his hand and sounded with a small thump on the sandy floor. "What the fuck is this? Am I tripping, or is your hand a fern?"

Mervin saw the shock in Soda's eyes and his own terror escalated. The thought that this was all a hallucination vaporized when he realized Soda also saw the stalk. Mervin recognized the screams he heard. They came from him.

Walking in tentative steps, Soda focused his attention on the stalk. The tendril swayed in an odd rhythm.

"Help me, man," Mervin said. Tears ran freely down his face.

"Sure, Perv," Soda answered. "We're not going to let some little prick from a weed ruin this weekend, right?" He took another step forward. The stalk reared back, ready to strike. "I think whatever the hell that thing is wants a piece of me, too."

Mervin yelped in pain as Soda sat on the end of the bed.

"Sorry, bud," Soda said. He reached for the first aid kit at the foot of the bed.

Mervin felt a flash of anger, as if Soda somehow caused this. The pain and panic unlocked old memories and resentment. Mervin remembered how Soda always seemed to be present when bad things happened in college.

"Just do something, man," Mervin said through clenched teeth. *Remember when Soda pantsed you in front of your parents on homecoming weekend?* "Hurry up about it."

"What do you want me to do?" Soda picked up his dropped bottle and drained the remaining suds. "What, exactly, do you propose?"

"I don't care. Just get this freaking thing off of me." *Remember how he used to laugh at all the part-time jobs you had to take, making fun of you for not having a trust fund?*

"I don't see a lot of options here, Perv. I could sail back for some help, you know."

"Don't you dare leave me alone," Mervin said. The stalk swayed over his hand like a charmed python. *What about all those girls he slept with just to prove he could? Even some of his friend's girlfriends.* "So help me, I'll hunt your spoiled ass down and kill you if you leave me."

"I figured you'd feel that way." Soda reached in his shorts' pocket and removed another beer. He opened the Red Stripe, took a long drink, and held up the bottle to offer Mervin a swig. Mervin declined with an angry shake of his head. "Maybe we should just cut off your right hand and make a run for it. Of course, that'd effectively kill your sex life."

"Fuck you, Soda! I'm not exactly in a joking mood right now." Mervin suppressed the urge to kick Soda off the end of the bed. He tasted hate like stomach acid in the back of his throat.

"All right, already. I was just kidding around, you know. What do you think of me trying some of that tropastiary shit here?"

"What?"

"You know – trim that son-of-a-bitch up so it looks like a giraffe or a gerbil or something – tropastiary."

"It's topiary, you dumbass."

Soda stood, the shifting of the bed causing another jolt of pain in Mervin's hand. "Whatever," Soda said.

He opened the first-aid kit, removed a pair of scissors, and snapped them several times, clapping the blades together. The stalk coiled back and sprung, lunging for the scissors. Mervin felt the burning again as the stalk elongated. It cracked like a whip when it recoiled. Soda jumped, howling in pain. The scissors flew from his hand, landing harmlessly on the bed. Soda grabbed his hand and clenched it to his chest. He looked at Mervin in terror, paused for a moment, then bolted out the open cabin door.

"Get back here, you piece of shit!" Mervin yelled. "Don't leave me alone with this!"

He picked up the scissors with his free hand and attacked the bed. He repeatedly stabbed at the mattress, picturing the scissors entering Soda's eye sockets. The bed spewed feathers, creating a surreal storm.

"If I get out of this, I'm going to kill him," Mervin said through clenched jaws. "I'm going to cut him up and feed him to the sharks. I'll let his boat – check that, his daddy's boat – sail away and say he never got here. That rich, piece-of-shit coward is fucking dead."

Soda entered the cabin again, a hatchet in hand.

"I had to get this off the boat. I think we need something bigger than those scissors."

A hatchet, huh? I'll put that to good use if I get out of this.

"How we gonna' do this?" Soda asked.

"Do what? What are you thinking?"

"Exactly." Soda inched forward taking baby steps. He held the hatchet in ready position above his head. "Do you think I can get that thing? I mean, well…Maybe cutting your hand off ain't that bad of idea. I don't think I can get close enough any other way."

Mervin went numb as he assessed the situation. Soda walked to the other side of the bed, putting some separation between him and the stalk. He picked up the bloodied shirt that Mervin had worn earlier and threw it to Mervin's good hand.

"Wrap one of them tourniquet things around your arm."

"Are you fucking crazy?"

"Just in case, you know. That thing…It looks pissed off or something," Soda said. "Wrap your arm, just in case."

Mervin's hand trembled as he wrapped the shirt about his bicep. He tied a knot the best he could with his left hand and his mouth. His right hand quaked violently on the bed and another tendril emerged from the bandage. He howled in pain. Soda screamed like a teenage girl at a horror movie, dropping the hatchet on the bed and again running out the door.

Mervin opened his mouth to scream "Fuck you," but the words never escaped. Another shoot, mature and hearty, erupted from the opening. Mervin gagged and watched the stalk grab Soda around the throat and take him down. Before succumbing to unconsciousness, Mervin saw the other stalks from his hand join the attack on the fallen Soda Pop McStain.

* * *

He stood taller now, enough to sway with the cooling ocean breeze. Glaring at the bungalow, he felt it taunting him. His appetite again escalated.

The sun moved from noon to afternoon, and began the evening setting. He spent the day focusing on the bungalow, waiting. His thoughts deteriorated. The two planes diverged into hundreds. Images came in jumbled pulses, and the only constants were confusion and hatred. He latched onto the hatred like a lighthouse in his brain's storm of bewilderment.

The horizon melted into the sea, and he realized how much larger he was. He possessed the ability to control his arms some. He studied his hands as if he'd never seen them before, but one of his many threads of thought remembered them. His hands made fists, giving him a new freedom.

Night grew. His hunger thrived and his hatred strengthened. He glared at the bungalow door, urgency itching in his insides. His hands caressed the new skin, exploring the form he'd become.

Morning's light swallowed night's darkness. His new form squirmed in anticipation. He turned to the dock, knowing something had changed.

His quarry laughed as they tied the catamaran to the dock.

* * *

Mervin awoke, all evidence of his human body gone. His stalks slithered, crawling over themselves in some type of botanic orgy. The cabin's humidity created the ideal breeding ground. The tendrils climbed the walls and covered the sand floor. They crept over the only remnants of Soda: his Hawaiian shirt, Bermuda shorts and expensive sunglasses. Not even a blood stain marked his memory.

Without any eyes or ears, Mervin still saw and heard from every leaf, bud and flower that comprised his new body. One brain no longer controlled him, rather every cell thought on its own. He felt no remorse, no mourning, for his former life. He understood his new situation instinctively - that somehow he'd happened on immortality; so long as he had a food source to sustain his new self.

From outside the bungalow, voices sounded. His stalks scurried to the window for a look.

"Perv, you didn't have to live up to the nickname, man," said some distantly familiar voice. Mervin watched through his thousands of eyes. Three men gathered out front. He recognized his former body, now naked and anchored to the spot from where he pulled the weed the previous morning. The two other men represented some significance in his subconscious, but he now cared little for them. He felt only hate and hunger.

Stalks shot forth from his former body. They wrapped around the newcomers' necks, attacking their faces. The screams were muffled by the slithering stalks swelling inside their victims' open mouths. His former college buddies dropped to their knees, floundering in a convulsive tango. More shoots erupted from his human form. They shot into eyes; into nostrils; into ears. They searched for other entry points.

Mervin's hunger dissipated.

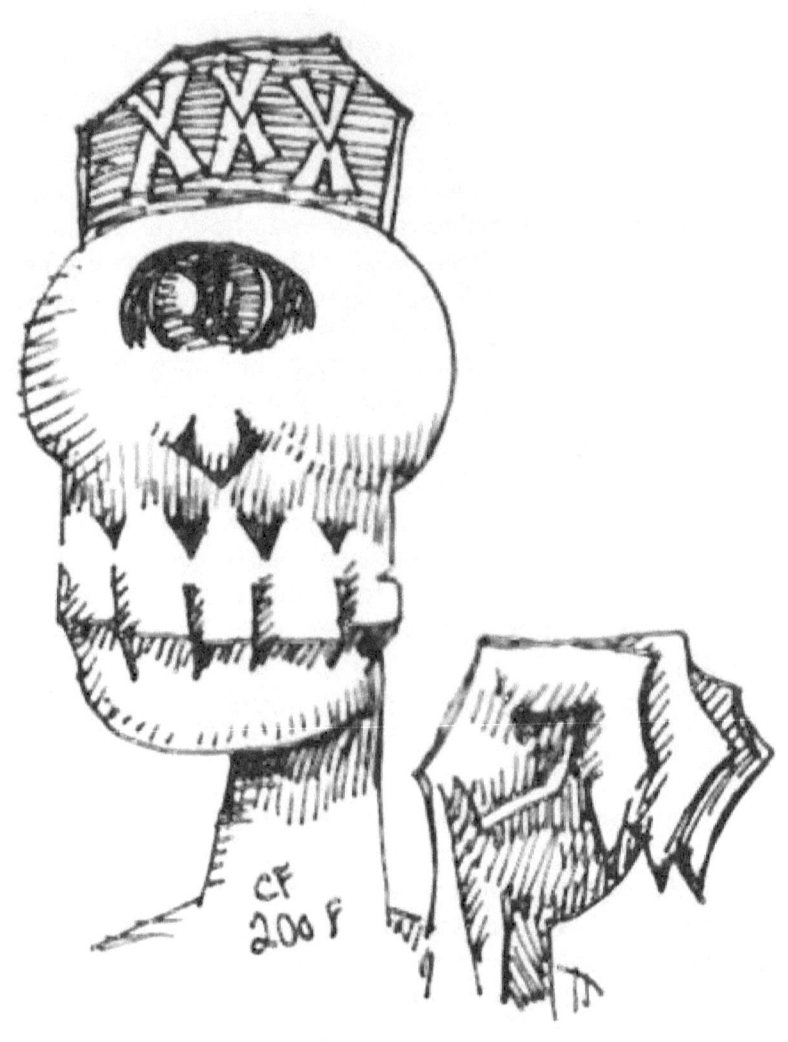

by David Dunwoody

It was like a giant teardrop. Like a giant teardrop that had fallen from the heavens and – immediately upon touching the earth below – crystallized, retaining its rounded shape and its translucent, liquid quality. Thus, the mystery sat solid upon the ground and bade curious Man to come a little closer.

The size of a small building, the teardrop was to be the cradle of modern civilization, for the men who discovered it had no explanation for its being and therefore attributed it to the gods. They erected towers and walls around it, fought wars for dominion over it, slaughtered babes before it, and pressed trembling red palms to its cool surface.

In the era when our story takes place, such pastimes as human sacrifice had been shrugged off, regarded as quirks of a more innocent age. Though the gods still ruled on high, Man now had science to elevate himself among the deities who had so long ago confounded him with thunder and meteors and eclipses.

Yet they were still confounded about the teardrop.

And still they feared it.

The ruling government had turned on itself. In a bloody coup d'état, the Prime Minister had been slain and his entrails slung from the highest spire of the highest palace in the nation. Those who hadn't had the benefit of advance notice, and those who failed to flee the country were caught in the midst of a guerilla war. Both armies were quick to establish rape and torture as their tools of the trade.

A nation burned, a nation no more. And in the smoke-filled capital city, behind massive walls tinged with flame – the teardrop sat silent, impassive, guarded by the Royal Army in the childlike belief that protecting it would protect those who had lived and groveled and died in its shadow since Man's infancy.

One morning, in the city square, a soldier patrolling the teardrop noticed something unusual. It was something about how the sunrise struck the side of the thing, the way it played unevenly across its milky surface...

There was a crack.

The soldier ran from the square, across the street, and into the Ministry.

Moments later, all the government's remaining ministers had assembled in the Great Hall to address the crisis.

"Just how large is this 'crack'?" demanded the Minister of War.

"Is it spreading?" bellowed the Minister of Justice.

"I don't think so--" began the soldier, before a collective glare silenced him and drove his meek form from the room.

"We need to know what *caused* it," said the Minister of Science. "The teardrop has been rocked by earthquakes, struck by lightning, and shelled by the Eastern Provinces, and never has so much as a blemish appeared on its surface!"

"How do you know that an outside force caused the crack?" asked the Minister of Religion.

"Just what do you mean?" the Minister of Science snapped.

"Perhaps," the Minister of Religion said, hands upturned, "it was an *inside* force."

The Minister of Science scowled, as he often did in the other man's company, and turned to the Minister of Justice. "I suggest you and I put together a team of investigators –"

"Why?" growled the War Minister, his face turning red. "Do you think this was a deliberate act? An act of subversion...?"

"Until we know the exact cause, it should be treated as a criminal investigation," agreed the Minister of Justice.

"Before you turn a holy icon into some sort of lab experiment, you should allow me time to pray over what's happened." The Minister of Religion glowered at the others. "Don't you think that this may very well reflect the state of our nation? Don't you think that the gods have seen the atrocities in the hillsides, the cities, in this very Ministry –"

"Of which you have been a part," snapped the Science Minister, "as much as anyone else!"

The Minister of Religion fell silent.

"We'll simply examine the crack," assured the Justice Minister, "*without* defiling the teardrop, *without* causing a panic in the streets. We'll examine it, then regroup and decide on the next step."

* * *

At twilight, they gathered in the park, surrounding the teardrop. The War Minister brought soldiers in from the city outskirts to provide extra security. Whether it was for himself or the teardrop, the Justice Minister wasn't sure, but it did little to ease the group's trepidation as they approached the icon with their guns and tools.

The Minister of Religion began to murmur platitudes. The Minister of Science wanted to get out of earshot, but he was captivated by the sight of the crack: maybe six inches long, paper-thin, starting up near the tapered point of the icon.

Then it spread.

Rapidly, the fissure stretched from top to bottom and began to widen; beads of milky fluid appeared at the edges of the tear and ran toward the ground.

"What's happening?" Someone cried. They all looked at one another. There was no answer.

The earth was trembling. The War Minister ordered his troops to train their weapons on the teardrop. The Minister of Religion let out a sharp cry and flung himself against it. "You shall not! Lower your weapons! I order you!"

The War Minister only laughed. "Shoot him!"

There was a second's pause in the city square, as the Minister of Religion's eyes searched for those of his comrades in the dark, and as each turned his face away.

He was cut down by a young boy in oversized fatigues. The bullets ricocheted harmlessly off the teardrop's surface and spun haphazardly through the Minister's body, shredding his insides and pulverizing bone, sending gouts of blood from his lips that choked off his last prayer.

The ground ruptured, and things began to emerge from the grass like bone tearing through flesh. They were thick, root-like, black things that rose high into the air, over the soldiers' heads. The Minister of War screamed for his men to fire, but it was hardly necessary.

The giant limbs rising from the earth bent, like a great insect's legs, and strained. Then the teardrop itself, that horrible fractured mass, was lifted up.

Those who weren't fixed in place by sheer terror, looking through the teardrop with thousand-yard stares, scrambled toward the Ministry. The only minister who stayed behind was the Minister of Science. He watched in horror as the rest of it came up out the ground – the rest of the Spider, with her cluster of blank, lifeless eyes, and her eight massive legs spanning the city square. Her egg sac, pulsating white, split open over the Minister's head.

The teardrop had ruptured.

A galaxy of white liquid exploded into the air like an orgasm – like some idiot-god's throbbing member spewing thousands of gallons of syrup earthward. Every inch of it was teeming with tiny translucent squirming things that the Minister recognized just before they struck him.

Spiders.

A million little white spiders.

Their wet, kicking legs filled his eyes and nose and mouth and he was driven back into the earth. They smothered him. He was drowning in them, and every time an air bubble entered his lips, it was pierced by the invading limbs of one of the creatures. They did a mad dance atop him, as if half-aware of their own existence and entirely unaware of his. They knew nothing of life, nor of Man, nor how their Mother had been worshipped through the ages by a race of fools.

The Minister of Science's lungs threatened to burst. His head was filled with an oppressive blackness, and his thrashing arms and legs went limp. He was only vaguely aware of his belly being slit open, of something fist-sized wriggling into his guts, and of something chewing voraciously through the lining of his stomach.

The soldiers, likewise, were knee-deep in newborn spiders. They blasted madly at them with their machine guns, but the mother, swaying overhead, a thousand babies still clinging to her belly, saw what was happening. Lowering her head, she began snipping soldiers in half with her mandibles.

The other soldiers turned their fire on her. She lumbered slowly towards them, exhausted from her labor, but nevertheless managed to sink the razor tips of her mandibles into the flesh of each trooper. She skewered their sternums, punctured their hearts, and tore out their backsides in a shower of gore.

The Minister of Science rose from the sea of newborns. His guts draped over his legs as the babies fought for purchase inside his belly. A thick, pulsating lump stretched his throat. It vanished up into his skull, and blood jetted from his eyes before the orbs themselves burst free, slapping against his cheeks, hanging by cords of nerve.

A tiny spider's legs reached tentatively from his eye sockets and waved in the air. The others retreated from his insides, dropping back into the teeming horde.

The Science Minister began to walk, unhindered, toward the Ministry.

* * *

Inside, the remaining soldiers had barricaded the entrance and stood at the windows, firing at anything that moved. And *everything* was moving; the ground outside was a slimy white carpet drawing inexorably closer to the building.

The Minister of War kneaded his hands, pacing back and forth behind the firing line.

"We have to get out of here!" cried the Minister of Justice. "Call for a chopper! We'll head to the roof!"

"We're not leaving!" roared the War Minister.

"You're not," replied the Justice Minister, and ran.

The War Minister drew a pistol and fired at the coward's back, but missed. It didn't matter; no one would leave the city alive. This was judgment. The Old Ones on high had grown weary of Man's cursing and complaining and had come down, as he always knew they would, to cleanse the earth and start anew.

The doors bowed inward, the barricade falling to pieces. Soldiers who tried to flee were gunned down by their commanding officer. He forgot about the menace outside and began shooting his own men, screaming all the while, *"NEVER RETREAT! NEVER SURRENDER! NEVER RETREAT! NEVER SURRENDER!"*

A moment later the doors fell in, followed by a gelatinous blob of shrieking arachnids – by the gods, they were shrieking – and the Minister of War collapsed on the steps and awaited his glorious demise.

It was not to be. A hundred little mandibles gnawed at his gut, but he couldn't die. *He couldn't die.* They scissored him open and made room in his belly. He felt tendons and arteries sever and organs pass along to be dumped out on the floor and devoured. He even felt one of them in his throat – *BY THE GODS!* – until it filled his mouth and nostrils with its legs and drove its jaws up into the prize.

* * *

The Ministers of War and Science observed as their fellow newborns redecorated the building. They strung inedible parts through crimson skulls and dangled them from the balconies overlooking the lobby, leaving those babies without hosts to swim in the nurturing blood below.

"Have you seen the cellars?" asked the Science Minister, eyeballs swinging jocularly.

"I have not," managed the War Minister; it was difficult to speak when half his face had been sloughed away.

"It's a literal abattoir." The Science Minister was obviously impressed with his host's vocabulary. "They have women down there, most barely of breeding age. Many with child."

"Keep the pregnant ones and give the rest to the troops," said the War Minister.

The Science Minister cooed. "Yes, sir. You're enjoying having all those medals on your chest, aren't you?"

"These?" Prying them off with a disdainful look, the War Minister tossed them to the masses. "No, it's these memories...memories of bloodshed and conquest and strategy. It all seems very exciting." Frowning, he pulled open the waist of his jeans and looked quizzically at the erection stabbing upward. "I don't know what *this* is for," he muttered, and pulled it off. It made a nice meal for the chattering infant at his feet.

The Ministry shook as the Mother slammed into it, her muscles and mind atrophying as death took hold. "We should move her away from here if this is to be the nest," said the Science Minister.

"See to it, then."

The War Minister cocked his head, teeth falling from the hollow in his cheek. "I just thought of something. I'll be back."

He made his way up to the roof, feeling a dull ache in his joints and back. He would need a new host soon. It was a shame, but at least he'd be able to take the man's memories with him. Such wonderful memories. Blood again rushed to his groin, only to pool in his trousers.

The Minister of Justice was huddled behind a turret, eyes searching the horizon. He'd long ago lost hope, the War Minister could see that much. The man was sitting in his own shit and babbling prayers he didn't believe. He barely registered the War Minister's approach.

"You're...you're not him."

"No."

"Are you going to make me like you?"

"No."

The War Minister pulled a bloody pistol from his jacket. "You are – were – the Minister of Justice?"

The man began sputtering, pleading, but his words went unheard. "And yet you were the one who had the women arrested and brought here. Under what pretense? Ah, yes. To 'protect' them from the guerillas. When rather, it was to rape them while you sent their fathers and brothers and sons to die in the hills, the cities."

The Justice Minister tried to get up and slipped in his excrement. He let out a hoarse cry, said something – "*Why?*"

"Why, you say?"

The War Minister paused.

"There are no gods," he told the trembling, sobbing shell of a man before him. "There is no morality. Not even logic. There is *nothing*.

"Why have I decided to kill you?" The Minister of War shrugged and took aim. "Who knows?"

And fired.

CF 2008

THE LEGLESS ONES

by Jodi Lee

A long time ago, this island was inhabited not only by the fae and the men, but also by every creature ever imagined. And you know, maybe there were some that most mortals *didn't* imagine, too.

Not everyone could see those creatures, of course. The fae could see everything, and the half-fae could see most things. Only the very gifted of the men could see past their livestock. If they'd been able to see the wings on the cows and the horse-like tails on the chickens, how would they have reacted?

But … they could not see. That's how we get to the story of The Legless Ones – three beings that once had legs. Before they raised the ire of the Good Father, that is. Their mother, D'ana, really should have kept a better rein on them. The Good Father kept her so busy, though, she had to leave the newborns in the care of their siblings.

* * *

The boys were born on a cold evening in the midst of the lambing season. A fog had rolled in from the hills, and the meadows were peaceful but for the occasional bleating livestock. D'ana and her consort, Allathair, had been busy visiting all the farms of men, blessing the ewes and lambs as they dropped. It was in the midst of this that D'ana felt a tug at her womb, and one, two, three, there they were. Allathair patted each on the head, told them to behave and, as all divine beings seem to do, moved on with his work. D'ana took the boys to the mounds under the mountains, where she and Allathair had made their home.

The other children glared at the newcomers. A sound like water rose in the room as the twin sisters, Boann and Sinann, cried out in protest. They were the oldest and would be stuck caring for the three ugly boys their mother had brought home. A brilliant light dazzled the eyes as Lugh and Luna added their complaints.

D'ana raised her hand and the room darkened as it fell quiet. She told the older children they must care for the new siblings, but that the three boys would have to go out and make their own way in the coming months, just as their older brother and sisters had done. She showed her children how the boys had grown, even in the few minutes since they'd entered the mound.

Grudgingly, the siblings agreed to watch over the triplets, even though they were rather ugly. Boann and Sinann secretly blamed the rolling fog for the triplets' conception, claiming some man had cloaked himself in it and managed to bed their mother whilst Allathair slept. Lugh laughed, sending showers of golden light from his head as he did so. He pointed out that the boys had four legs and tails, though - that they couldn't be of the men, who only had two legs and no tails.

Luna smiled at her new brothers, thinking to herself that they resembled the dragons who danced the fields in fall, after the harvests. Of course, the others would never have seen them. Sinann and Boann didn't like walking the fields, and Lugh never went out at night. Still, she didn't want to get stuck making sure the three stayed out of trouble. As her mother turned to leave the mound, she hid herself in the voluminous robes and made her escape.

She managed to get to the horizon before her mother noticed her and scolded her. Showing only half her face, Luna remained rebellious and rode the skies for the rest of the night.

Meanwhile, the three older siblings faced the three youngest on either side of the dinner table. When the triplets opened their mouths, a horrible screeching echoed through the mounds, rather than the language all deities are born knowing. Sinann recoiled when she saw their tongues were thin and forked. She rolled her eyes as she left, and Boann quickly followed; but not before silencing the triplets with a douse of icy water.

After the sisters had gone, the triplets started up with their cacophony once more. Lugh covered his ears, and yelled at them to shut their mouths. In the end, though, Lugh guessed it was only fair. His sisters had taken care of him when he first arrived, and now it was his turn. He didn't have anything else to do anyway – at least for several hours. He watched as the three identical boys began eating items off the floor.

What could he do to keep them occupied while he slept?

An idea came to him then.

"You three, come here. Tell you what... you're hungry and I'm no good at gathering food. There are farms around here with lots of interesting things to eat, so why don't you go out and find those? Don't forget how to get back here, and don't come back until you've each eaten three chickens, three piglets, and three lambs."

Lugh covered his ears again as the boys discussed their options. They really couldn't eat Lugh (and were glad he couldn't understand what they were saying, as he was still bigger than they were) and they *were* hungry.

Two turned to the door, while the third turned to Lugh, and nodded. The third then followed his brothers outside, and off they went, the sound of Lugh's laughter following them.

The three roved the countryside, pillaging whenever they came across a yard with livestock. Not long before the dawn crept over the edges of the mountains, the triplets returned to the mound to find Lugh snoring.

Lugh awoke, startled not only by the noise of his brothers' return, but also by their condition as they stood over him. Each one was covered in soupy animal blood, and one had the partially gnawed remains of a chicken stuck in his hair. Lugh's eyes passed over the boys in turn, and he realized they were now just as tall and broad as he.

"Clean yourselves before Mother and Father see you," he said, and left them to it. He had business of his own to attend.

In a flash, Lugh was gone, only to be replaced by his sister, Luna. Looking the boys over, she groaned, but helped them get cleaned up. Sinann and Boann entered the mound only moments before their parents, and none were the wiser – the triplets were as clean and strange looking as when they were born, only much bigger.

They were now full grown.

D'ana took them in her arms for a hug, and then settled them in for a nap before she took them out to meet their neighbors. These, of course, were the lesser gods; the boys would have to learn to accept their homage.

Thus passed the first day of their lives.

Early in the evening, Allathair and D'ana left the mound to tend to their blessings. Sinann and Boann followed not long after, swearing Luna and Lugh to secrecy without giving their youngest brothers a second glance.

It wasn't long before Luna melted away, and Lugh was once more left with the four-legged siblings.

"You three did so well last night, why don't you go out and find yourselves some more fun tonight? You might want to go out farther, though. You sure did cause a stir among the men!"

All three nodded their assent, and removed themselves from Lugh's presence. They didn't like him anyway – the room always seemed too hot when he was home.

* * *

Many months passed, and D'ana was confronted by Allathair early one evening while they blessed the fields.

"The men are beseeching us to find out what is killing the livestock, my love. I think we both know what has happened. Don't deny you have had the same suspicions. The youngest of our brood have created a serious problem, and we must act."

"Allathair, I can not believe any child of ours would cause such destruction and dissent. Please, can we not look elsewhere first?" D'ana wrung her hands as she spoke to her husband. Not only did she have the same suspicions, she'd actually caught the boys during one of the raids. What they'd done to the cattle had been frightening, even to her.

"No love, act we must, and now it must be." He took her hand and led her behind a large mound. He comforted her briefly before turning her head so she could see the havoc taking place in the pasture beyond.

When D'ana nodded, Allathair moved past the mound and called out to his sons. The only response they gave him were three identical sneers as their teeth tore into an old plow-horse. The animal screamed in pain, and Allathair was forced to act. He quickly stepped closer and held out his hand, muttering in the old tongue.

The horse stilled, but his children whined and hissed in protest.

"You have broken the laws of our people, all three of you. We've tried to teach you to eat what is given you by our subjects, but you've taken from them the very gifts that sustain us. You will be punished!" Allathair's voice boomed out over the fields, causing Lugh to cower behind a rolling fog. It caught the attention of Luna, who hovered closer to her family. Boann and Sinann came to stand by their mother where they could snicker at the trouble the boys had found themselves in.

"You – old man. Mussssn't interfere. Can not. We needssss the Mother. Sssshee lovessss usssss," three voices responded to Allathair's words. All the boys moved as one, as though to strike their Father down where he stood.

D'ana stepped out then. When they saw her coming towards them, they slunk backward, hissing to themselves. The cadence to their unapologetic voices broke her last hope of salvaging her family.

"I stand with your Father. You have done wrong. Face your punishment properly, as befitting your status!"

"No!" the boys cried, in unison. "You lovessss ussss, Mother! Do not interfere. We musssst rid the land of the creaturessss!"

Faster than any being on the island, the triplets traveled to their Mother and snatched her up. Allathair wasn't quite quick enough, and was left standing with a piece of torn shift in his hand. Anger built within him, anger he could see mirrored in D'ana's eyes.

The two had been together for so long, they no longer needed to communicate verbally. They were gods, after all.

Allathair lowered his head and looked up at D'ana from under his heavy brows. She, in turn, closed her eyes and began chanting in the old tongue.

Sinann and Boann ran off, leaving little trails of water where their tears had touched the ground. Luna dashed behind the fog as Lugh had done, although she dared not go to him for comfort. Everyone knew Lugh had been goading the younger boys on, and he might be the next one punished.

Allathair waited a beat of his heart, then joined the chanting. The triplets hissed and struggled, letting D'ana go free as they thrashed about on the ground. With a final grunting scream, they collapsed at Allathair's feet. No longer were they seven foot tall with the legs of a beast. Now they were on their bellies, wriggling with no limbs at all. Allathair picked up the closest triplet, wrapping his hands around the beast's slippery, writhing neck.

"You would rid the island of the creatures living upon it. From now on, you will rid the island of the mice and rats and whatever you can catch and swallow whole. You will have no legs to run, and must slide on your bellies. You will have no teeth to chew, but only fangs with which to hold your food as you swallow.

"You will be as the worm, only above ground. Man and animal will fear you, and you will be alone. So be it."

With that, Allathair released the creature, and the triplets worked their way through the tall grasses, disappearing into the field. D'ana wrapped her arms around Allathair's generous waist, and sheltered her face on his chest as she grieved for her lost children.

* * *

Many years later, the three were banished once more. Only this time, they were driven into the sea. Perhaps killed, as no one has seen them since. Legend has it that there are many in other lands.

Seeing is believing, but I am old and not likely to travel far.

Perhaps you will witness what lies beyond!

To Feed the Little Children

by Sharon M. White

Lydia stood just beyond the glow of the sodium-arc lamps as men serviced their tractor-trailer trucks in the safety of the light. The truck stop and diner stood alone, facing a winding two-lane road and towering rock cliff. The mountains were at her back, shrouded in mist, and a river whispered by in its shadow. Rain misted down like tiny pieces of a nearly forgotten dream.

I need to get on with it. Lydia thought, watching the gritty-looking men with their hard eyes and mean laughs. She looked down at her baggy shirt. *This body is too small, too angular, and bony. I feel confined.* The thin pants stuck to her skin and her long, wet hair stuck to her cheeks.

What a mother will go through just to feed her babies.

Lydia hoped to speak to the body-weaver after she fed her children. The skinny, achingly small bodies the weaver had given her were becoming a bother as her true form wanted a bit more freedom.

Waiting a moment longer in the darkness and rain, she thought of her children to focus her energy on the task ahead. Small and nearly helpless, Lydia knew she must supply her little ones with proper nourishment or they would perish. Motherly devotion finally moved her in the right direction. "Here we go," she muttered to the weeping sky.

As she emerged from the shadow, the congregated men nudged each other and tossed catcalls at her. Most of them were harmless, and she wasn't looking for harmless. The vile one lurking in their midst was the grand prize.

The smell of danger, like a gossamer thread, lingered in the air. It carried a spicy citrus tang, and mingled with the scent of hot food from the diner.

The fragile human body she wore wanted what was in the diner, while the devilkin inside her wanted the source of the other odor.

Lydia inhaled, sorted the different smells, and honed in on the tangy aroma of hot, half-spoiled oranges. Turning toward the tempting scent, she saw the man standing between two trucks. Half his face hidden in the darkness, and the other half was lit by a sickly yellow street lamp. A chill traced down Lydia's spine, making the fine hairs bristle on her arms.

The man smiled and nodded to her. With a shy smile of her own, she returned the nod, and quickly lowered her gaze, playing prey to his predator. A game Lydia loved.

The smell of frying meat drew the human Lydia toward the diner at the far end of the store. She had no doubt that he would follow. The truckers' voices fell to a drone in her head and she slowed her pace, so the man could follow her through the shadows.

Silently, Lydia thanked the body weaver, knowing he had been correct in choosing her new body. The homeless waif look never failed to snag the attention of the vilest man in the group That didn't make the tiny shell any easier to wear, though.

Lydia began reaching for the diner's grimy door when a large, warm hand squeezed her shoulder. Fighting back a grin, she allowed her muscles to sag, imitating submission to a stronger force. The man's pleasure at this was evident, the way the tangy, acrid aroma grew thicker around him.

"Hey, there." The man gently turned Lydia so they faced one another.

The other truckers were stereotypical, what with their bulging bellies, hard-lined faces, baseball caps, flat asses, and pick-up lines, but this man looked nothing like a typical truck driver. He had a gentle, lineless face, and a trim, muscled body. Even his voice sounded softer and more trustworthy in comparison.

Lydia allowed him to pull her away from the door, and near the shadows his smile faltered on his taut face. The tip of his tongue played with a divot on his upper lip. His eyes darted from Lydia to the parking lot, then to the diner door, and back to Lydia. When his pupils dilated, little iron butterflies fluttered in Lydia's midsection, making her feel nauseous.

Stay in control, Lydia. Don't lose him now. He will be divine and well worth the wait.

The man clasped Lydia's fragile hand firmly as soon as they were out of the truckers' sight. "You hungry? Here all alone?" He nodded in unison with Lydia, already knowing the answer. "You're soaking wet, sweetie. Come with me, and I'll fix you up right and proper. I've got food in my truck. It's a sleeper-cab, so you can eat, sleep, and get warmed up."

Keeping his eyes glued on her, the man gently led her to his truck.

No one seemed to notice what had taken place.

Lydia's jaws clenched, and her saliva glands pained in response to the sting of the man's scent. She had to force her physical self to the forefront, and repress the part of her that was born in darkness – the part that wanted to devour his screams, to feed on them, and share the divine buffet with her growing babes.

Lydia let the man wrap a satin-trimmed, purple fleece blanket around her shoulders as she sat on the bed and ate a cooling burger and chips. The man introduced himself as Bob, and Lydia didn't press for more information.

After finishing her meal and accepting a bead-filled dog that smelled like cotton candy, Lydia pretended to fall asleep.

A snap-down shade that matched the truck's leather interior rattled over the back window as the man climbed into the driver's seat, and started the engine.

The physical Lydia did fall asleep, but the cunning succubus inside her peered through half-closed lids at the man. Every few minutes, he would turn to look at the sleeping form. The enticing spoiled-oranges smell grew stronger with each stolen glance. The bounce and wobble of the moving truck kept the human Lydia – the Lydia he found so attractive and desirable – sleeping like a baby.

After an unidentifiable amount of time, the truck stopped. The CB radio shut off and the rock music died. Moments later, the man's

51

voice was in Lydia's ear.

"Sweetie, do you want some candy? I've got some candies for you up front."

Lydia opened her eyes slowly, and watched him go to the passenger's seat, to retrieve a large paper sack from a compartment under the dash. Candy fell onto the seat beside him as he retrieved the bag. Melting chocolate mixed with citrus and she lunged for the mountain of tempting sweets.

Lydia bent near the seat, plunged both hands into the bag, and sifted through the chocolate. The bulge of the man's crotch brushed Lydia's cheek as he stood up. He shuddered and gasped before continuing to the bed.

"Baby, bring me a sweet, would you?"

Lydia's stomach churned with the iron butterflies once more, and she nodded, picking out a white striped disc of chocolate for him. When she drew near, the man reached out and pulled her roughly between his legs.

"How old are you, dear?" he asked.

"Older than I look," Lydia replied. Her voice, only a whisper, was nearly lost in his heavy breathing. The man let go and she backed up a space, licking chocolate from her fingertips.

"You're so young and pretty. Here, sit with me." The man patted his knee and smiled, but quickly became irritated when she didn't move toward him. "Come on. I fed you didn't I?"

When Lydia didn't respond, he snagged her shirt and yanked. He turned her by the hips, and pulled her roughly onto his thigh so she straddled it, her back against his chest. The silver candy wrapper drifting to the floor held her attention.

As the man pressed his face into her hair and inhaled, Lydia drew a deep breath through her open mouth and tasted his sin. She tasted the fiendish longings that would soon satisfy her craving for black energy.

Lydia heard the zing of a zipper, and let the stillness take her again. The rhythmic motion of the man's free hand (and his moans) let her know what he was doing as he groped her. The orange spice of his excitement tinged the air, and mixed with his sweat.

Lydia's stomach tightened, roiled as the demon begged to be loosed. Suddenly, the kneading and pinching stopped, and the heavy arm pulled her tight against his heaving stomach and quivering thigh muscles.

"I'm going to let go and I want you to get down on your knees right here," the man said, pointing to the floor between his feet without letting go of her.

His grip loosened, and Lydia slid from his leg and planted her feet between his, staring wide-eyed as he moaned and pulled and stroked himself. Oranges overwhelmed her senses, and the demon raged as the man neared the peak of his excitement. Soon all his energy would be at the foreground of his mind, where it would flow into his screams.

"You know what I want you to do, honey?" he panted, like someone on the last leg of a marathon. His mouth hung open, and his tongue quivered on his top lip, teasing and heating his passion even more. Half standing, he wriggled his ass, and let his pants drop below his knees. His grunts only lightly veiled his laughter.

"Yes, I know what you want," Lydia said. "But you have to give me head first."

She felt the scales cover her downcast eyes, and the skin bulge around her shoulders.

"Oh, it's not nice to tease, little girl. And here I was hoping you weren't old enough to even know what that meant."

The man didn't even look at Lydia as he scooted himself to the edge of the bed and reached blindly for her with his unemployed hand.

"Who's teasing?" she asked, her voice filled with a hundred whispered screams.

Those words were enough to get his attention, and the reaching hand stopped mere inches from its intended target, fingers splayed. The stroking ceased, and he looked up with wide eyes and an open mouth. His fleshy pink tongue still worked at his upper lip like a vulgar, flexing slug. As his gaze fell upon her, Lydia saw the fear in him, relished it a moment, and allowed her body to finish changing.

First, wings burst from her ribs. Bone and tissue exploded, pelting the interior of the cab, and her skinny arms shed their flesh, melding into her new appendages. Her finger bones changed to claws that curled and uncurled, and she voiced a long, ear-splitting scream. Her small breasts extended, pulled upward, shuddered, and split apart, to reveal bony hands and two new arms, leathery and full of ropy muscles. Her eyes bulged under the scaly lids, and jellied down her pale cheeks. Her new, larger hands grasped her splitting skull and pulled it free, and her new head grew to the size of a small basketball.

Lydia dropped the used, little-girl skull and stretched her wings. After giving them a good ruffle, she turned to the man and shivered in anticipation, sucking in air through her new nostrils.

Tears ran down the man's face, and violent tremors shook his body. Lydia laughed. One scaly, black, hand gently lifted his chin. "It's not nice to tease me with those tears," she said, before her fingers clamped down on his bottom jaw like a vice. "I want to hear you scream before you give me head."

The man wailed as her grip tightened. Lydia leaned close and sucked his screams into her lungs. The sepia wings that stretched behind her quivered as his screams fuelled her hunger. Muscles bulged and thrummed under her black hide as she grew, stretching and reshaping her new body. The screaming stopped, and Lydia gazed into the man's watery brown eyes.

"Don't make me. Please, let me go," he whimpered.

"Oh, yes," Lydia growled. She planted a dry kiss on his bulging cheekbone.

"Kill me. Just don't –" the man's words were mashed as Lydia's index finger and thumb punctured his cheeks. His face caved in on itself, making his eyes resemble a cartoon character who just realized he sat on a live bomb.

The man's bottom jaw unhinged, and his cheekbones snapped, sounding like twigs being twisted as they gave way under the pressure.

Lydia opened her mouth wide, let her purple, twisted tongue slide out and dangle suggestively in front of his face until she heard a scream sprout in his chest. Then she slid her dripping tongue up his neck, and moaned into his ear:

"Don't tease. It's not nice."

With her free hand, Lydia grasped his forgotten manhood and gave a little squeeze, until his building scream burst into her waiting maw. Her claws inched slowly into his groin, causing a fresh spate of squeals to fill her mouth and nose. The man's eyes rolled back, and showed only white.

"Give Lydia some head now, sweetie," she purred.

Unfortunately, the man's screams had been reduced to whimpers filled with tears.

Lydia's tongue hardened and shot through his thick neck, breaking his spine and snapping the tendons in two. Blood gurgled from his mouth. The barbs on Lydia's twisted tongue sawed through the muscles as she thrust and pulled for several minutes, moaning in ecstasy.

Finally, the man slumped forward and hit the floor with a leaden thud. Holding his severed head to her chest, Lydia screamed in triumph, shook her wings, and clawed the truck floor in a macabre victory dance. The thrill ebbed quickly, though, and Lydia dropped the man's head beside his body, pissed that he couldn't scream for her again.

Filled with the energy from Bob's dark fantasies, Lydia climbed out of the truck, and flew to a clearing near a tree line.

In the gathering darkness, she could sense other beings closing around her. Chatters and clicks erupted from every direction, and a grin pulled the corners of her mouth, to show her carnivorous teeth. A legion of feet shuffled from the shadows, sounding like a forest of dead leaves caught in a gale. Lydia's sepia wings extended until the tips touched, and the night fell silent.

"Come and replenish yourselves, my children," she said.

A flock of tiny imps rushed under their mother's amber wings to feed. Carefully she crouched to her knees, and called to the babes who were still hiding in the foliage. Soon every feather tip rested in the mouth of a deviling. The babes suckled and grew until Bob's energy was gone from Lydia's body.

"Go and grow strong, loves. This world is a bounty for us all," Lydia grinned.

The children squeaked and cried out to her.

"I'll return soon," she said, stroking one tiny, upturned face. "You'll have to wait till then."

Lydia flapped her wings, and her children scurried back into the shadows.

Curling into the fetal position, she wrapped her body in her wings, and the demon goddess shrank and disappeared under the stiff feathers.

* * *

The next day, the sun smiled across the eastern mountains, and a steady wind rushed to meet the light, peeling away the layer of feathers that clung to Lydia. The young woman lay on the ground, beautiful and dainty, blanketed by her lengthy jet-black hair.

The epitome of innocence and frailty.

Waking to the caress of the wind, Lydia pushed herself to a

sitting position, stretched her arms, and wiggled her slender fingers in front of her eyes. She inspected the new form, stood, and smiled as her ebon hair cascaded to her waist.

She liked the new body, with its elegant beauty and slenderness. The last body had been too skinny and angled for her liking. Nevertheless, she knew the smaller and more helpless she appeared, the more likely she was to find the most deviant men – the ones filled with the darkest energy.

Hunger pains rumbled as Lydia skirted the tractor-trailer, and stepped onto the rutted pavement beyond. The road shimmered in the morning sun, and Lydia saw the silvery glint of a car approaching.

A man stopped and offered her a ride, a nervous smile twitching his thin lips, and Lydia detected the tangy spice of a hidden fantasy in his breath. She smiled as she slid into the front seat.

Her children would be eating well tonight.

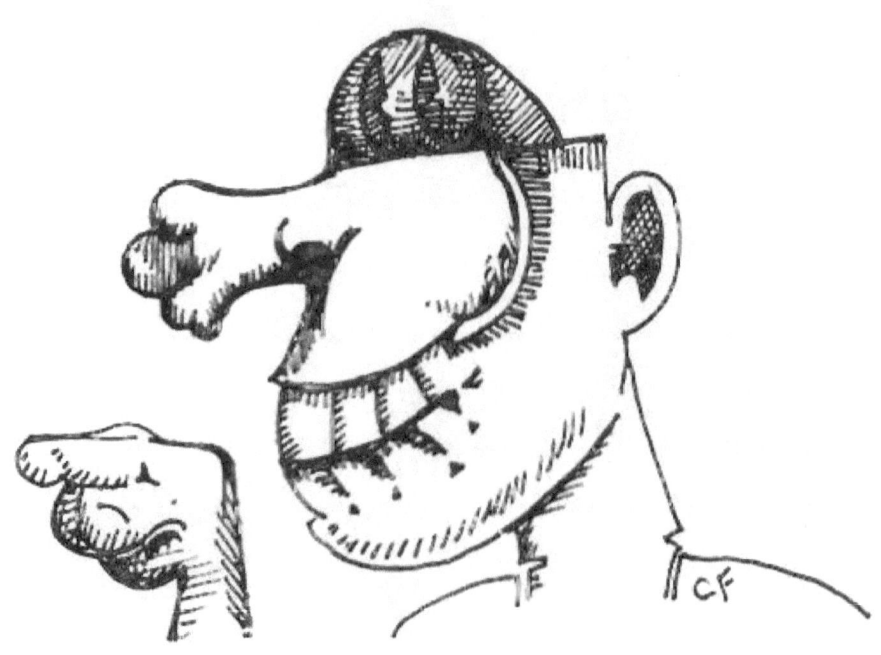

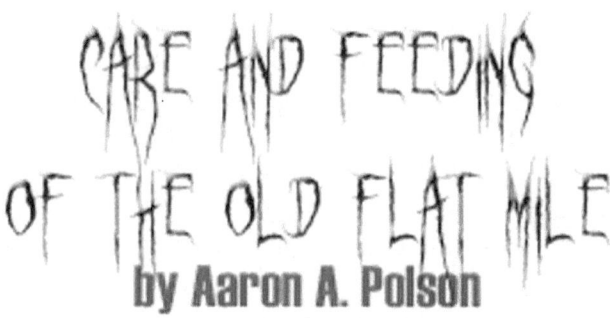

CARE AND FEEDING OF THE OLD FLAT MILE
by Aaron A. Polson

I

Some places were just born evil, and the Old Flat Mile slid easily into that description. Constructed shortly after the Second World War, that stretch of road was originally intended for glory. Architects and businessmen pointed to what they dubbed the "Golden Mile" as the linchpin in Springdale's future rise to prominence. The luxuriant homes built there were sure to draw investors with the deepest of pockets. That was the plan until little Calvin Unruh was crushed under the tracks of a bulldozer while chasing his brother's errant throw.

Construction halted immediately, investors clambered for their money, and the proposed housing development disappeared like a summer mirage. The county took over the road, dubbed it North 1800, and left it unpaved. The locals christened North 1800 "Flat Mile," surely with no pun aimed at poor Calvin's unfortunate accident.

Meanwhile, Calvin's older brother, Daniel, lived with the knowledge that he threw the football his brother chased that day. He spent many years as a haunted, pale boy with black eyes. And as Daniel grew up, the road waited.

In time, Daniel's guilt faded. Especially after he eased into his teen years and developed a penchant for tinkering with engines and blondes. Some said he tried to forget his brother with those fast cars and girls, and maybe they were right.

Daniel loved to drag race, and the level stretch of the Flat Mile was the perfect spot to flex his automotive muscle. There were other times, quieter evenings with full moons, during which he would ease his '57 Chevy down that road to put his girlfriend in the mood.

On one of those nights built for romance, he steered onto the Flat Mile only to find his buddy, Jeb Harwood, waiting in his own hot rod, itching for a race. Something in the rumble of those two cars must've woken the road; it had tasted blood once, and its hunger must've grown.

Daniel ended up losing control on a patch of loose gravel, and the race concluded with his '57 wrenched around a tree. His girlfriend survived, eventually moving to Kansas City, marrying, and raising three children. Daniel, however, never really left the Flat Mile.

Unfortunately, Daniel wasn't the last to smear his young blood in the dirt and sand. Teenage boys, full of hot blood, loved to prove their mettle with fast, reckless driving. After a few more fatalities, city officials blocked off the Flat Mile, and the road was left in loneliness and disrepair.

Over the next forty years, stories faded, signs were taken down, and the road slept. Eventually, a new generation of Springdale teens found a use for North 1800.

II

Oblivious to history, Jimmy Campbell, tried to navigate his father's Chrysler through the thick April mud of the Old Flat Mile while his girlfriend, homecoming runner-up Maggie Bloch, complained. Beneath them, the road smelled engine exhaust, purred with the sweet rumble of a straining engine, woke, and called its children home.

"What the hell were you thinking, Jimbo?" Maggie asked. Her long fingernails carved deep into the smooth faux velvet bench seat as the car groaned, its wheels spinning in place.

Jimmy's beefy paws clutched the steering wheel, gripping so tight that his knuckles turned white. "Look, I figured it hadn't rained in a couple days, so it'd be okay."

"Well, a couple of dry days don't matter much when it rains for a week straight."

Jimmy ran a handful of stubby fingers through his sawed-off brown hair. "Hell, I thought the full moon would be sweet."

Maggie wasn't ready to play nice. "Real romantic," she said, glancing out the window and catching a ghost of her own, thin-faced reflection in the glass. "It isn't even a full moon."

"Like hell." Jimmy released his foot from the gas, and the car sighed with relief. He pushed his face against the windshield and searched for the moon.

"No, it's only about three-quarters."

"Awww," Jimmy moaned, dropping his head to the steering wheel. "I wanted to, you know, do something you might think was romantic." His hands dropped to his chin. "I really fucked up. If the Charger was ready, we wouldn't be stuck."

Maggie's face broke into a smile. "You think your dad's old clunker could get us out of this mud pit?"

Jimmy's face sprouted with red blotches. "First of all, it's a '69. A classic, not a clunker. And *no* it couldn't get us out of the mud. Once I get that puppy humming, I'm not taking it out in this stuff, anyway. If the road was dry, hell yeah. I can't wait to —"

"What? Spin out on the flat mile and end up in the ditch?" Maggie shook her head and brushed her auburn hair away from her face, pulling back into a loose ponytail. "Listen, sweetie. You get me out of this mud-hole, and I'll make sure we find a dark, quiet spot for some real romance." Her hand slid onto his lap, and stroked the inside of his leg.

Jimmy slowly straightened in his seat. He glanced at Maggie. "I love you, babe."

"I know." She smiled, but her face suddenly dropped into a stunted frown. "What the hell was that?"

"What was what?"

"I saw something move behind you." She shivered. "Look, the sooner we get out of here, the better."

"Don't freak on me."

"I'm not, I just …want to get back to town, okay? Civilization?" She waved her fingers toward the blue glow of Springdale. "I don't like this road. The stories —"

"— are mostly silly legends to scare kids; to keep people from driving too fast."

"Well, they're working. I'm scared."

"Right. I'll get us out of here, then." Jimmy pushed his door open with a squeak of rusty hinges.

"Where are you going?" Maggie's voice eked out with a taint of panic.

Jimmy had slipped from the car, but momentarily ducked back into the dim glow of the dashboard lights. "Just going to find some wood or something I can wedge behind the tires. You know – for traction."

"All right," she said slowly. "Just hurry, okay?"

"Don't worry about it. I'll be back in a jiffy."

Maggie jabbed the automatic locks as soon as Jimmy slammed his door. She huddled on her side of the car, feeling a bit chilly in the April darkness. *If he would just hurry*, she thought. She twirled a bit of hair on her finger. *This place is creepy, but the old full-moon trick is kinda sweet. He's a —*

Maggie's thoughts were interrupted by a loud bang on her door. Jimmy's face hovered just outside her window.

"Gotcha," he muttered, loud enough to be heard through the glass.

Maggie snapped the door open, smashing it across his knees. "Damn it Jimbo, I nearly wet myself." She stood up next to the door, and looked into the darkness, past her doubled-over boyfriend. "Jimmy …who's that?" she asked, shivering.

Jimmy let a pathetic little groan slip out of his mouth as he rubbed his knees. "Just some guys. They can help push the car."

Three figures shimmered in the moonlight. They appeared to be teenage boys, somewhere between sixteen and nineteen, but they all seemed strange. Their faces were pinched together, too gaunt and pale, even in the moonlight. Maggie tried to muster a friendly smile, and the boys' lips cracked open in response. They wore dirty clothing, streaked with dark stains.

Most likely mud, Maggie thought. *Gross.*

One stepped forward and stretched out a withered hand. His fingertips were stained black. "I'm Dan. This here's Lonnie and

Earl. We can help," he said. Maggie couldn't see his lips move. A taint floated with his voice, like the sound of a light wind cutting through a strand of old trees. The other two stood behind him like chimps; the one introduced as Lonnie poked a finger into his mouth and scratched at his gums, digging out something black that shone in the moonlight.

A rancid odor oozed off the boys. It was wet and fishy – the scent of a riverbank after a flood.

Maggie quickly slipped into the car and slammed the door shut. Jimmy said something to the three, and sloshed through the mud to the driver's side. He tried to shake the thick muck from his shoes before shutting the driver's door and slipping the gear shifter into neutral, but it was no use.

"Who *are* those guys?" Maggie whispered. She caught herself with one hand against the dash as the car lurched forward. The back of her neck burned like some dull razor had plucked out the hairs one by one. "I haven't seen them around school."

Jimmy shrugged, maintaining a solid grip on the steering wheel. "Probably home-schooled or something."

"Home-schooled? Really?" Maggie cast a curious glance at Jimmy's profile. "They look a little freaky to me."

"Yeah, well, some of those home-schooled kids are religious fanatics, you know. Maybe these guys are part of some wacky cult. They seem nice enough, though."

Maggie turned to look over her shoulder. The yellow faces of the three strangers grinned in the back window, showing bent and browning teeth. Their eyes were cold and black, so she quickly snapped her eyes back to the front of the car. "They make me feel *dirty*. The way they *leer* at me."

"Babe, if they're religious zealots, they probably aren't used to seeing hot numbers like you. Really." Jimmy leaned over and kissed her on the neck. Maggie pushed him away and flashed a tepid smile.

"Look, we're almost there," Jimmy announced. He straightened in his seat and peered into the cone produced by the headlights. "We still on for that dark, quiet spot?"

"I'll think about it," Maggie muttered, crossing her arms across her chest. She couldn't shake the crawling sensation of the boys' eyes on her back.

"See, safe and sound," Jimmy said as the headlights lit up the yellow sign at the end of North 1800. "I'll just thank them, and we're off."

"Jimmy, don't …."

"Just a quickie. They really helped us out of a jam."

Jimmy stepped out of the car.

Maggie stared at her feet for a moment, looked at Jimmy's open door, and slowly brought her gaze to the window next to her. A flat, leering face with bloodshot eyes and stretched, chapped lips floated an inch from the window.

"You're purdy," the face gibbered, its voice muffled and cold. Maggie let out a small gasp, quickly turned away from the window, and reached for the door lock. Her thumb flicked the switch, but the lock wouldn't cooperate with Jimmy's door hanging open.

Jimmy poked his head into the car. "Hey, Maggie. This guy owns a '57 Chevy—stock *everything*. They other guys have nice rides, too. Vintage. They say I should come out sometime, race with them."

"That's nice, Jimbo. Once you get that old jalopy of yours running again, anyway." Maggie's voice crawled with sarcasm. "Can we *go*?" she implored. She heard a slight scratching sound.

Outside Maggie's door, pale fingers felt for the handle.

"Yeah. Just a sec." Jimmy's face vanished again, but Maggie still heard his voice. "Look, is there anything we can do to thank you?"

Maggie's door popped open, and she nearly collapsed in the mud. She would have, if not for the strong arms that caught her. She plucked at them with her fingertips, feeling cold, wormy flesh — they way she imagined the white belly of a catfish would feel just after it was pulled from the river.

Maggie's mouth dropped open, but no sound escaped, as a rotten hand slipped across her lips. Another set of hands moved over her body, and she squirmed against the invasion. Jimmy's face was pale in the darkness, and she only saw him in profile as the arms dragged her into the thick, swishing grass around the ditch.

"You see, buddy," Dan said to Jimmy, once Maggie was several yards away, "we've been out here a long time. Too long, really. Your girl there … she's pretty. Earl, Lonnie, me — we've been dead a long time, but those urges just don't go away. It's real lonely out here."

Jimmy turned to the car, and caught a glimpse of Maggie's flailing feet as Dan's greasy companions pulled her further into the grass. His stomach dropped, his heart throbbed frantically, and something big and hard crashed against the back of his head.

Dan stood over him holding a rusty tire iron. He bent down, breathing his filth on Jimmy's prone form. "Don't worry, buddy," he sneered. "We'll take real good care of her." Then, he raised the tire iron, and cracked it repeatedly against Jimmy's skull, until blood and brain matter leaked out.

When he finished, he drug Jimmy's body to the ditch and joined his friends across the road.

And so, the Old Flat Mile filled its belly on hot, young blood once again, while its children enjoyed a feast of their own.

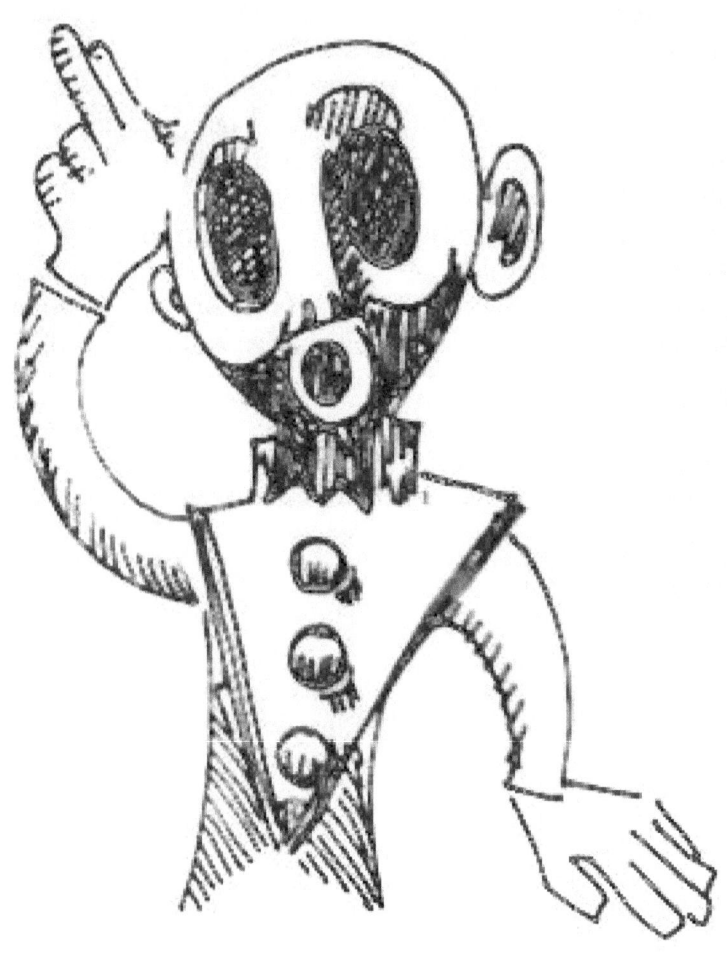

by Allison M. Dickson

Mark lay awake, his eyes shut. The starch-stiff sheets in his hotel room carried the salty, illicit aroma of sex. His hand rested on Mitzy's shapely thigh – a woman who slept deeply beneath the blankets, her light snores drowned out by the rattling drone of the room's air conditioning unit.

A bar of late-afternoon sunshine found its way through the lone window's vertical blinds, and lit upon Mark's eyelid. He turned away to squint at the clock on the bedside table. It was three-thirty, and he needed to be on the road by four if he hoped to make it home before nine.

"Wake up, Mitz." He stroked the cheek of the sleeping beauty beside him. She stirred briefly, muttered something that sounded something like "fifteen more minutes," and rolled away from him.

Mark pushed the covers back and swung his legs out of the bed, his muscles groaning in protest. Mitzy inspired him to perform sexual acts more suited for men half his age, and he didn't realize what kind of a toll it was taking on his middle-aged body until he stopped moving for a few hours.

He grinned over his shoulder at Mitzy's sleeping form, her head buried under a pillow, dark brown hair a matted mess. The sheet had fallen low on her body, revealing a small sunflower tattoo on the swell of her hip. He had to turn away before the temptation to kiss that flower became too strong.

Mark opened the cheap oak-and-brass end table drawer to remove his wallet, phone, and wedding ring, which Mitzy always had him remove during their meetings. Even though he didn't share the same sentiment, he was happy to humor her. Mark's ring, like his marriage, meant nothing to him. What he shared with his wife was nothing more than maintenance of a material lifestyle, and whether it was an accurate assumption or a defense mechanism on his part, he believed Carolyn felt the same way.

He flipped open his phone to check for missed calls, and noticed a text message from his wife instead. He hated when she did that.

He had never been a fan of texting, finding it both tedious and annoying, what with its spelling and grammatical shortcuts. The only reason he carried a cell phone was for convenience while he ran his sales routes, and the following message exemplified his distaste for text messages.

need 2 talk. call me when u get this.

Mark flipped the phone shut, tossed it carelessly onto his pile of clothes (which had been shed hastily the night before), and retreated into the bathroom. When he returned, freshly showered and back in his suit, Mitzy was out of bed, and stood before the dresser mirror. She'd pulled her hair into a neat ponytail, and was using the corner of a wet wash cloth to clean the smudged makeup under her eyes. News blared from the room's small TV set, effectively killing any remaining sexual ambiance.

Mark kissed her on the cheek as he went to zip his small suitcase. "I'm heading out, sweetheart. I need to hit the road if I want to be back in Portland at a decent hour."

"I know," Mitzy replied. "But I wouldn't count on that. Look." She nodded toward the television, which showed an endless line of cars snaking down the north and southbound lanes of I-5. "A tanker drove off the overpass, and came right down on the freeway. There's fuel everywhere. They're saying it won't be cleaned up until sometime tonight."

"Fuck." Mark sat on the end of the bed in a huff.

"My thoughts exactly," Mitzy said, turning around and straddling his lap. The shine of her freshly-washed face made her look a decade younger. "We can just stay here, and you can get out first thing in the morning. You wouldn't mind actually spending the whole night with me, would you?" She said this between kisses that started on his mouth, and worked down his neck.

"That sounds like a great idea, Miss Mitzner," Mark smiled. He lay her down on the bed, and began pushing her dress up, revealing the body he fantasized about day and night. The jarring ring of his phone stopped him before he could go much further.

"Oh ignore it, baby. Don't stop now," Mitzy pleaded.

Mark planted a kiss on her mouth. "Can't. If it is who I think it is, I need to answer it." Then he leaped up, and jogged to the bathroom. It was his wife, as he expected.

"Hello?" he said as he closed the door.

"Hi hon. How is your trip going?" his wife chirped.

From the sound of her voice, he could tell she was in an excellent mood, which was odd, because Carolyn seldom deviated from her cool serenity.

"Busy. Productive. But I'm looking forward to coming home," he replied.

"And I'm looking forward to having you. I know you're going to have a long trip back, though. I've been watching the news."

"Yeah. I'm thinking I might head back in the morning, instead of sitting in that mess all evening," he sighed.

Carolyn cleared her throat, and her voice took on a cold edge. "You don't have to take the freeway, Mark."

"You're right. I don't," Mark admitted. "It would've been a hell of a lot more convenient than trying to find a route through Washington's back roads, though."

His wife sighed as if she was talking to a willfully ignorant child. "That's what Aria is for, sweetheart. I got her *specifically* for this sort of thing. Frankly, I don't know how a man in your profession can go without her."

"Aria" was the name she'd given to last year's Christmas present – a fancy GPS navigator that could mount on a windshield or dashboard. It was the sort of pretentious luxury that irritated his sensibilities beyond reason. His sense of direction had always served him well, and on the occasions it didn't, he always had his road atlas.

Currently, "Aria" rested in the trunk of his Lexus, and he was happy to let her rot there.

"Honey, I've done my job for twelve years without having to rely on that silly gadget. I'll come home as soon as the freeway opens back up," Mark said definitively. "Now, is there a problem or did you call to start a fight?"

"Oh, *I* don't have a problem with anything, Mark," his wife said. Her voice darkened, and Mark felt a chill creep up his spine. "Although, I'm sure if you decided to leave now, Sarah Mitzner would be awfully sad."

Whatever strategy Mark had devised for navigating his way out of the skirmish with his wife was obliterated, and he sat in stunned silence on the edge of the motel's dingy bathtub. The truth, hidden for a year, had risen to the surface like a nasty boil, and was on the verge of bursting. He felt a flash of anger at being called out in such an embarrassing manner, but it was never his wife's style to broach a subject gradually.

"Well, at least you simply shut up and didn't jump immediately into a lie," she continued. "How could you think I wouldn't find out about this, Mark? Sarah's father has been a colleague of mine for twenty years. I knew I'd married an emotional wet napkin, but I just didn't know you were such an idiot."

Her voice remained as placid as a pool in a monastery garden, as if she'd rehearsed every line, while Mark remained planted on the tub's edge, the right words eluding him. He knew she was prepared for any response he could come up with.

"I do think it would be a good idea for you to get home as quickly as those Washington back roads will allow, though. Rain is expected tonight, and I would hate for all your things to get soaked in the driveway."

Mark leapt up from his seat, his silence finally broken by her increasing vindictiveness. "Goddamn it, Carolyn! You don't have to use the scorned woman routine. I fucked up royally. You heard it from me first. Would you rather get divorced over the phone right now, or should we handle this like adults?" His mouth had dried completely, and a cocktail of anger flooded his body.

"That's up to you, Mark. If you want to come home before your shit gets soaked, so be it."

Carolyn's final words made Mark's stomach roil. For a year he'd carried on his secret romance, and a part of him had even wanted to get caught – to have all of the ugliness out in the open so he could leave Carolyn with a clear conscience. Now, at the prospect of confronting his wife's icy fury, he was ready to go back into hiding.

He used to love Carolyn for her ability to govern her emotions. She was a smart and quick-witted woman, and he rarely had to deal with nagging or tears. Even in the face of devastation, she was a pillar of stability. For the last few years, however, he'd begun to view that controlled exterior as a complete lack of emotion.

A gentle knock sounded at the bathroom door.

"Mark? Is everything okay?" Mitzy asked. She seemed worried.

Mark opened the door and stepped out. "No, but it will be," he said. Pacing through the room to make sure he hadn't forgotten anything, he spied his wedding band on the end table, and picked it up.

"She knows, doesn't she?"

"Yes." He didn't know what more to say.

"Well… that's a relief, isn't it?"

"Yes and no. She's never been one to shoulder bad news well. We'll have a lot to talk about when I get home tonight."

"Tonight?" Mitzy said. "But I thought you were going to stay. Don't you think it's best she knows? I mean, you don't want to drive upset, and you're never going to accomplish anything while she's so angry. Besides, we have nothing to hide now, right?"

Mark shook his head. "Mitzy, I have to go home. Carolyn's holding my possessions for ransom. The longer she has to sit and think, the more vindictive she's going to get. I need to sit her down and reason with her before she calls that pit-bull lawyer of hers."

"Okay. You win," Mitzy seethed. Go home and make nice with your wife so you can keep all your toys. That seems to be what this is really all about."

Mitzy turned away began throwing her toiletries a little harder than necessary into her travel bag, her mouth drawn into a thin white line.

Mark sighed. Mitzy was Carolyn's polar opposite in every way. Unlike Carolyn, Mitzy was prone to vacillate between every emotion on the spectrum during the course of a single conversation.

"Come on honey, don't do this!" he cried. "I'm only going to be home long enough to say what needs to be said, pack my things, and find a place to stay. I'll call you as soon as I'm out, which will probably be sometime early tomorrow." He turned her around and kissed her on her forehead. "Okay?"

"I've given you one year already. What's another day when you're in love with a married man?" Mitzy growled. She shoved her feet into her shoes and slung her bags over her shoulder.

"I'll call you. I promise," Mark said.

Mitzy didn't look back as she stalked out the door.

Once all Mark's bags were shoved in the trunk of his car, he walked to the motel office to drop off his key. In truth, he could've left it on the room table without stopping by the main office, but he wanted a moment to cool off before heading out.

"Some mess on I-5, ain't it?" the clerk mumbled, when Mark approached the front desk.

"Yes. I have a long drive ahead of me, I guess."

The clerk nodded, giving Mark the sort of look a parent might give an ornery eight-year-old. "Hope you have an alternate route planned, mister. If not, you might as well check right back in. Heck, I'll hand you your key back right now, if you want."

"I can't," Mark said simply. "I have … an emergency at home. The sooner I get on the road, the better."

"You headin' north or south?"

"South. Portland."

The clerk whistled between his teeth and hitched up his pants, like a man intent on lifting a heavy piece of furniture. "Well, I suppose you could take the Stevens Pass Parkway east, pick up 9 South down through Snohomish, and follow that until you reach I-405 …"

Mark nodded impatiently as the man prattled on about a section of roads and towns with which he only had a passing acquaintance.

While Mark had been to Seattle frequently enough – mostly to see Mitzy, but also to meet with his distributors – he'd rarely ventured off the main arteries, so he knew he'd be giving his road atlas a good workout this time.

"Best of luck, buddy," the clerk said finally, ending his lengthy dissertation. "You'll get home. Probably around midnight, but you'll get there."

"Thanks" Mark replied. "I need all the luck I can get." He gave the clerk a wave, and walked back to his Lexus. The atlas would be in the pocket behind the passenger seat. He'd plot his route based on what he could remember of the clerk's advice.

There was only one problem: the atlas wasn't there. Mark felt the pocket behind the driver's seat. It was also empty.

After feeling under all of the seats and becoming increasingly irritated, he decided to check the trunk.

The Rand McNally was nowhere to be found. He tried to think about the last time he used it, and came up blank. It had been awhile. "Shit," he exclaimed under his breath. He supposed he could pick up a map at a gas station, but that would take time and money.

About to close the trunk, he spied a familiar white box.

Aria.

Mark almost slammed the trunk door right then, but after he paused to consider his options, he reached in and grabbed the GPS anyway. It was his only hope of getting home before the rain drenched all his belongings.

In the car, he unpacked the unit, plugged it into the cigarette lighter, and turned it on. It didn't take long before a husky female voice with a British accent spoke to him.

"Hello. Please enter your destination."

When Carolyn had first given him Aria, he'd toyed with the gadget, and entered in a few preset addresses. He selected *Home*. Aria responded by saying: "Calculating route."

She pronounced "route" like "root."

"So cultured, aren't you honey?" Mark spoke to the GPS aloud, feeling a little silly in the process. He pressed Aria's holding bracket onto the windshield, snapped her into it, and started the car.

"Travel three hundred feet and turn right," Aria instructed.

Mark had known it was going to try to put him on the freeway.

"Oh no, sweetheart. We're not doing I-5 today." He stopped to adjust the GPS's settings, and successfully programmed it to bypass freeways. The device was very simple to use. He admitted to himself (begrudgingly) that it was a bit more efficient than the Rand McNally.

"Recalculating route. Travel three hundred feet and turn left."

"Much better, Aria," Mark said. He waited for a few minutes for traffic to clear, and swung the Lexus onto Eighth Avenue.

"Travel 3.2 miles and turn right."

Aria's color display showed the progress of Mark's car through the city with startling accuracy. He flipped on the radio and uncovered Kurt Cobain, belting out "Smells Like Teen Spirit."

Before long, he found himself singing along, at least to the parts he could understand clearly.

Then, in the middle of the final chorus, Aria spoke up again with her snooty British lilt. "Travel one mile and turn right."

"Thanks for the reminder, ma'am," Mark said, in his best attempt at British pomposity.

"Yes, of course," Aria replied.

Mark's heart took a small dive.

Did the machine actually respond to him?

Pulling onto the shoulder, Mark turned his attention to the GPS that hung from the windshield. Re-routed traffic buzzed by as he plucked Aria from her mounting bracket and cradled her in the palm of his hand. The avatar that signified his car had stopped moving.

"Travel one mile and turn right," Aria said again, causing Mark to jump and nearly drop her.

"Fucking weird," Mark breathed, once he regained his composure. The GPS unit lay in his hands, and seemed to be functioning normally. Maybe he'd imagined the voice. He *was* under a considerable amount of stress.

With a small juggle, he got Aria back into position, and pulled onto the road. He couldn't afford to linger any more than he already had.

"Right turn approaching."

"Yes I know," Mark said, feeling irritable and edgy. He tried to forget the unit's little anomaly, tried to blame it on an overactive imagination, but it wasn't that easy.

"Turn right," Aria said pleasantly.

Mark rounded the turn marking Highway 2. So far, the motel clerk's route seemed sound. Aria was silent, and clouds overtook the clear sky, bringing to an end the Northwest's rare March sunshine.

The traffic on the country highway was surprisingly sparse, given the traffic incident, so Mark edged his car to a hair below sixty and set the cruise control.

"You might watch your speed," Aria said. Her voice had taken on a condescending tone – one that reminded him distinctly of Carolyn.

Mark felt his guts turn to jelly. Goosebumps lined his arms, and he reached up to loosen his tie. While he didn't have enough experience with the GPS to know its entire vocabulary, he was pretty sure Aria was not designed to judge his driving.

"That's it, Aria. You're weirding me out," Mark said, reaching down to Aria's power button.

"You might want to reconsider."

The machine's voice was cold, and Mark jerked his hand back as if it had been burned. "What the ... are you actually talking to me?"

Mark eased the car onto the shoulder again, and threw it into park. Rain spattered softly on the windshield, and he felt a screw turn in his gut. Aria's display had turned blue.

Reaching up, Mark tapped the machine with a shaky finger.

The three-inch screen then went black.

"Fucking thing is broken. That's perfect," Mark muttered. His voice was embedded with irritation, but in reality, it was actually disguising relief.

The next moment was a blur. Mark had been reaching out to press Aria's power button when a high-pitched electronic shriek had erupted from the unit. Mark had screamed, jamming his hands against his ears, and the GPS had flipped from black screen to blue screen, and begun playing what looked like a low quality video one might see on a convenience store surveillance tape.

Blinking, Mark leaned forward and discovered a figure that looked remarkably like his wife. The woman's hair jutted in every direction, as if she hadn't slept in days, and her housecoat flapped open, revealing her aging naked body.

"Holy shit," Mark breathed.

The woman didn't just *look* like his wife. She *was* his wife.

Mark watched in terror as Carolyn stumbled drunkenly into their bedroom. Her face wasn't clear, but he could see it was streaked with smudges of eye makeup, as if she'd been crying.

Mark leaned in even closer, fascinated despite of the impossibility of the situation. He couldn't recall a single day when his wife had looked so disheveled. "What are you doing, Carolyn?" he murmured.

Carolyn proceeded to open the drawer of his nightstand, and reach inside.

Mark's stomach became a pit. "No honey, not the gun."

The .45 automatic looked big in her hands as she placed it on her lap. She stared at it for a moment, and rubbed the barrel with the edge of her robe in slow, circular motions.

Meanwhile, Mark had become feverish in his seat. His shaking, sweating hand had wrapped tight around the gear shifter, and the windows had fogged over, turning the car into an opaque cell. His eyes bulged as his wife lifted the gun to her temple.

"No … Carolyn … don't you dare. Don't you dare!"

The Ruger's report filled the car just as the GPS's screen cut out, leaving him with the echo of the gunshot, and the placid idle of the Lexus' engine. Mark looked away quickly, breathing hard, his eyes squeezed shut.

"Okay. Okay. Wait a minute. Wait, wait, just wait." He kept his eyes closed in an attempt to clear his mind. "That wasn't real. That didn't happen. There's no way that could've happened. I'm losing it. I'm losing my goddamn mind." He fumbled in his pocket for his cell phone and dialed home.

"Pick up the phone, Carolyn. Pick it up," he said, rubbing his eyes, refusing to look at Aria, unwilling to admit what he'd seen.

Carolyn's smooth, professional voice answered. "Hello. You have reached the home of Mark and Carolyn Angstrom. We're not home right now, but we'll return your call at our nearest convenience."

Mark waited for the voicemail to end, and lurched into action. "Carolyn, pick up the phone if you're there. Please. I know I'm the last person in the world you want to speak with right now, but I need to know if you're okay. Are you there? Please honey, pick up the phone." He decided to wait a few seconds, even though he knew she was gone.

Willing his eyes upward, he saw that Aria's screen had resumed its map display, and he hung up the phone.

"Keep driving," ordered Aria. The sudden, harsh voice made Mark jump in his seat.

"Fuck you!" Mark cried, yanking the power cord from its socket. Only, the display remained on.

He tried grabbing Aria, intent on pulling her – bracket and all – from the windshield, when a sizzling current ripped into his hand and up his arm, throwing him back against the seat, and nearly knocking him unconscious. He slumped away from the navigator, stunned and gasping for breath, while Aria stared at him silently, just a harmless piece of electronic equipment.

Mark fumbled for his cell phone, and called Mitzy.

"Hello?" Her voice was flat, emotionless.

"Baby, I've got some major problems out here," he stammered. "It will sound too crazy if I tell you over the phone, but I really need you to come out here and pick me up."

"Mark, I'm tired of coming to your rescue. If you're in trouble, call the cops," Mitzy snapped.

Mark felt his mouth go dry. This was not the sunny woman he knew – the one he fell in love with.

"Mitz, please! I need —"

"I'm not giving in to you this time. I've been your back-up wife for a year, Mark. I don't have a ring or the ability to be public about it. Today was your chance to make good on us, but you made a fool out of me. I'm done, Mark. Goodbye."

She was gone before Mark could say another word.

What could he have said to change her mind? That he'd already called his wife and there was no answer, because he'd watched her blow her brains out through a possessed GPS system?

Mark closed his eyes. He wanted to run – to abandon the Lexus – but he didn't know where he could go. He was stuck on the side of a lonely freeway, for God's sake.

"Keep driving," Aria said simply.

"I'm done driving. Fuck off."

The GPS display flickered blue again, and came to life, revealing a grainy image of Carolyn, her body sprawled on their bloody, ruined bed. The picture changed without warning, and Mitzy sprung into focus. She was busy applying makeup in a mirror – the one Mark recognized from the vanity in her apartment. A dark, masculine shape moved behind her.

"Oh no. Not her. Please not her." Mark shifted in the driver's seat to get a closer look.

The man in the video leaned down and kissed Mitzy on the shoulder. She reached back and draped her arm around his neck, the way she did when Mark approached her from behind. But this man was a stranger.

"Turn it off!" Mark screamed at the display. "Why are you showing me this?"

"Keep driving." Aria said. The Lexus' engine revved, and the door locks initiated, trapping him inside. Mark pulled the handle, but it was stuck fast. "Drive, Mark."

With no aid from his hand, the gear shifter moved from Park to Drive, and the car quickly accelerated from the bumpy shoulder to the smooth blacktop of the highway. He screamed with surprise, grabbing the wheel and mashing both feet on the brake, but it was no use. The pedal sank lifelessly to the floor, and the wheel held rigidly in place.

"Travel one mile and turn right," Aria said, as calm and collected as she had been fresh from the box.

"Help! Let me out!" Mark pleaded in the steamy interior of his car. He let go of the wheel and began frantically pounding at the driver's side window. With the glass fogged, he couldn't see where the car was taking him.

"Travel one half mile and turn right."

Aria hadn't changed. The avatar on the display carried him forward in a straight line. There was no turn ahead on the map.

The Lexus's speedometer pressed past eighty miles per hour.

Suddenly the window defogger kicked on high, and the windows began clearing of their condensation, almost as if Aria wanted him to see where he was headed. The country landscape, blanketed in shadows, rushed by as the black Lexus picked up more and more speed. The needle of the speedometer was edging into three-digit territory when Mark gave up pleading and resorted to screaming.

"Travel one quarter mile and turn right."

Mark peered ahead with milky eyes and saw a floating freeway bridge – the kind that spanned Washington's many lakes. His mind snapped and became frenzied with terror.

"Stop the car! Aria! ARIA STOP THE CAR!"

In a last, desperate attempt to escape the commandeered Lexus, Mark pulled the handle on his door and rammed the full brunt of his weight against it. It wasn't enough.

"Turn right," Aria said.

Mark looked up in time to see the wheel of the car pull hard to the right. He was still screaming when the Lexus ramped over the bridge's low-slung railing at top speed, corkscrewed through the air, and landed heavily in the river.

As the car filled with water, Mark continued to scream, his throat hoarse, his fists broken and bleeding from pounding at the sedan's unyielding windows. Aria, on the other hand, was cold and unforgiving as the lake that was gradually swallowing them both. And she only had one thing to say:

"You have reached your destination."

ILL CONCEIVED

by Felicity Dowker

Meg slid the small cloth bag across the table to Ella, sipping her coffee and watching the other woman's reaction.

Ella stared at it. The red material had yellow crescent moons all over it; a drawstring held the bag closed. She could see the swell of whatever filled the bag rising beneath the material. She looked up at Meg.

"What is it?"

"It's a L'il Cup," Meg said, her voice gentle. "I know it may seem a strange gift, Ella, but I just thought that after all you've been through, it was time you celebrated your body the way that it is. These last three years have been hard on you, and it's time you allowed yourself to grieve."

Ella looked back down at bag, then back up at Meg. Her polite smile was tired.

"I don't understand. What's a L'il Cup?"

"It's a menstrual cup, Ella. Safer than tampons. Better for the environment. Cheaper. But the reason I got it for you was so you could celebrate your bleeds; get your fingers into them and commune with your cycles. Accept them. Know them. Own them."

I don't want to get my fucking fingers into my menstrual blood and commune with my cycles, you idiot. I hate my cycles – malicious fruitless things that they are. I want a baby. A baby, can you understand that? I know what you're trying to do. I know what you're all trying to do. You want me to move on. Well, I can't. I won't.

But all she said was: "Thank you, Meg. I appreciate the kind thought."

Meg beamed at her, and patted the bag.

"The instructions are inside. It's really very easy to use. You'll love it, I guarantee it! I've used one for, oh, well over twenty years now. It will help, Ella. It really will. And you deserve help."

Yeah, and you need help. The kind a psychiatrist offers, you demented hippy. If you weren't my husband's sister I would tell you where you could shove that cup; and it's not where you've been shoving it for the last two decades, either.

"How's Oliver?" Ella's question was pointed, and Meg had the good grace to blush.

"Oh, he's fine. Just fine. He's starting to walk, you know. Just a few doddery steps."

"Will you be having any more?" Ella's voice was icy now, and Meg swept a nervous hand through her hair.

"Oh! Um…Ella, do you really want…? I mean –"

"No. I don't really want to know. I don't really want to talk about it. I don't really want to talk about *anything*. I really just want to lie down."

"Of course! Of course, I'm sorry. I'll see myself out. I'll give you a call, ok? No; you'll be resting – I'll just speak to Jonathon. If there's anything you need –"

"Sure," Ella said, and Meg bustled out, wringing her hands. Ella saw the moisture in her eyes and didn't care.

Not one bit.

Go on, cry. Go home to your husband and cry to him about how horrible I am, while you cuddle your son and plan your future babies. Tell him how nice you were to poor broken Ella, how you gave me something to celebrate my dead useless eggs, how you told me to get my fingers into the blood that signifies my failure, month after month after month. Go on and cry while you congratulate yourself.

She took a Panadol and went to bed, and she was still there when Jonathon returned home from work at 6:30pm that night.

She closed her eyes and pretended to be asleep, and he stood there for a moment, looking down at her inert form on the bed through the deepening gloom. Then he pulled the blanket up over her, and gently pushed a tendril of hair off her forehead.

Fuck you, too, she thought as he closed the door behind him. *Fuck you and your healthy sperm. It must be hard having a reproductively crippled monster for a wife. You're so patient; you're a regular* saint. *Saint Jonathon, patron to the barren.*

Bitter tears stung her eyes, and she wept into the pillow, her hands crossed over her aching, hollow belly.

* * *

Such dreams, they had. Such plans. They had it all worked out.

High-school sweethearts, they married at 20, and enjoyed a decadent three week honeymoon in the Whitsundays. Ella spent those languid days in a white string bikini, the sun rippling over her oiled skin, her hair falling in straight sheets to her trim waist. She would pin Jonathon to the sand, narrowing her dark eyes in mock menace, pulling back her pink lips to show her small and decidedly non-threatening teeth. He would lay under her, flailing his neat hands in theatrical surrender, his face dense with the unshaven scrub of a man at ease.

He'd had no potbelly then; his flat abdomen tapered pleasingly down to his groin. Ella loved to run her fingers down the dark snail trail that began above his belly button and continued to a hidden place only his new wife could go.

They were so young, so happy, so unaware of the empty future that awaited them.

They agreed it would be foolish to start a family so soon. It was becoming fashionable to have a career first – there would be no chains linking Ella to the kitchen sink – and they were down with that fashion. They could dig it. Jonathon was already making a name for himself as an investment banker, and Ella had a promising future in insurance broking.

The world was their oyster. Children were not even on the horizon.

A decade went by, and still they agreed it was too soon. They had progressed in their careers and were bringing in a tidy sum of money every year. They owned a terrace house in a good neighborhood. They had shares. They had two cars. They went on annual holidays to exotic locations. They indulged in the latest household accessories. They bought a pug and named him Pig. They gardened. They drank wine on their porch with their smiling friends. They listened to music and went to festivals. They made love on Wednesdays and every other Saturday. They slept draped over each other like lazy cats.

They were happy.

And then, when they were 35, Ella woke up at 3:00am. Her hair was soaked in rancid sweat, her blood hot with urgency, her limbs shaking. Her biological clock had not just begun to tick; it had *exploded*, ravaging her body, mind and soul, and she *needed to have a child* now.

She had woken Jonathon and they had made love at once, Jonathon still blinking the sleep from his eyes and looking up at her in confusion as she straddled him; Pig the pug watching from his perch on the end of their bed. She rode Jonathon with a bright and jagged desperation, and he was terrified. When he orgasmed it was more a self defense mechanism than the culmination of his pleasure.

"We'll do it again tonight," she'd said as she rolled off him, panting. Her voice had been blank, and he had remained staring at the ceiling, not wanting to look into her eyes. He had a feeling they would be blank, too, and he didn't want to see that.

They did it again that night, and the next night, and the next night, and after a year of nights, they went to the doctor.

There was nothing wrong with Jonathon; the root cause of their childlessness was Ella, though the doctor couldn't say exactly why. A fertility drug with the encouragingly cute name of Clomid became their bosom buddy for the next 12 months. But Clomid was a fickle friend, who promised much and delivered nothing at all, and they found themselves back at the doctor's feet, begging for more help.

Then the IVF began, and the blankness in Ella's eyes never left again.

Three years of implantations, all unsuccessful. The financial expense was phenomenal. There was physical pain, but it was dwarfed by the agony they felt in their cracked hearts. Every time they swore they wouldn't hope. Every time they hoped anyway.

Every time their hopes were dashed, and every time it hurt a little more.

They never made love anymore. Why bother? It was pointless.

Jonathon's sister, Meg, gave birth to a boy, Oliver, a bundle of wide blue eyes and fuzzy blonde hair, and Ella considered simply picking the child up and running away with it. Changing her name. Bringing the boy up as her own. Perhaps killing Meg if she had to – if Meg would not let Oliver out of her arms.

Now they were 40, and all hope was lost. There would be no more IVF. There would certainly be no natural conception. Ella prayed for early menopause, but her periods came with hateful regularity, a vivid reminder of her unfulfilled potential, a whiff of fertility that might have been but never was.

Jonathon loved Ella with a weary but abiding depth, and Ella loved him in her own ruined way, which wasn't really any way at all. There was little of her left to give once you took out the energy she expended on hate, regret, self-loathing, anger, grief and longing. They were a sad and pale shell of a couple, united now more by their shattered dreams than by their shared joyous memories.

As gray snakes began to writhe in their hair and their skin began to droop and shrivel like their hearts, they clung to each other out of habit with cold dry hands, and they waited for purpose or death.

Ella hoped for the latter.

* * *

She sat on the toilet, the red bag peppered with yellow moons lying empty on the sink beside her, her underpants bunched around her ankles.

In one hand she held the L'il Cup. In her other hand she held the instruction pamphlet. She frowned down at the words, studying them, absorbing them. Meg was right; they were quite simple.

"Alright," she said, exhaling and bringing the silicone thing level with her eyes, "let's give this a whirl, you and me."

Push. Pop open. Twist. Done.

She sat motionless on the toilet, feeling shocked. She'd just had her fingers inside herself for the first time in…she couldn't remember how long. The fleshy heat had been foreign and overwhelming, and she looked down in wonder at her fingers, daubed with blood.

My dead egg. My dead baby. My blood.

A tear traced a silver track down her cheek. She stayed like that for a long time, staring down at her blood, imagining it pooling forlornly in the soft cup buried inside her.

"I love you," she told her bloody fingers. "I'm sorry."

* * *

"Mummy," the darkness cooed in her ear, honeyed and malevolent. *"Mummy, I'm waiting."*

* * *

Ella jolted awake and sat up, gasping for breath, the sheets twisted into damp whorls around her perspiring body.

Jonathon twitched in his sleep, moaning. She stared into the night for a long time before lying down again.

* * *

"What is *that*?"

Jonathon's face wrinkled in disgust as he watched her maneuver the full L'il Cup out from under her skirt. She'd become expert at it as the months rolled by. And, to her chagrin, Meg had been right about some other things, too. There was something about digging her fingers into her own body and seeing – *touching* – her own monthly blood that was…invigorating.

"It's a menstrual cup," she said, wiggling it around near Jonathon's face. He shrank back and she giggled. The sound was coquettish and weird in the small ensuite bathroom. "Are you thirsty?"

"That's disgusting."

"No, that's the stuff babies are made of," she said, and there was enough sharpness in her voice to make him leave the room without further comment.

She stared down into the cup.

It's beautiful…so beautiful.

The blood separated as it built up; the thin, straw-colored plasma was on top, and the darker syrup was below. It looked like an alcoholic shot poured in careful layers.

She loved to watch it as she tipped it into the toilet. The plasma merged with the water, leaving no trace; but the darker blood was a living, writhing thing. It tumbled in rich threads into the water, leaving a dancing path in its wake. It looked like chocolate sauce, then raspberry cordial, then a delicate roset; then it was gone as she flushed it all away.

Delicious things. It made her think of delicious things.

She let her tears fall into the water as it bubbled and spun her dead egg, her not-baby, out of sight.

* * *

"I'm tired of waiting, mummy. I don't like it. Tell him to hurry up. I'm getting angry, mummy."

The darkness was urgent, commanding.

"Who are you? I'm nobody's mother. Tell who *to hurry and do what?"*

"He needs to do it soon, mummy. He's making me wait and I don't like it!*"*

(Let me out! I don't like these dreams! Why am I having them? The air smells of rust here! It's wet, and cold! Oh please let me out! Oh please ...)

But it had called her mummy; and she had liked that. *Liked it rather a lot.*

* * *

Jonathon cast a glance at his slumbering wife. She was frowning and muttering in her sleep, but that was normal. Her rest had been unquiet for years. So had his.

Satisfied that she was deeply asleep, he slipped out from under the sheets and padded to their ensuite. Closing the door with care, he flicked on the overhead fluorescent. He looked down at the toilet bowl, a little ripple of revulsion at his own baseness raising the hackles on his neck.

I'm a man – no, not even that; I'm human. *I've got needs, and I can't – won't – bother Ella with them. Maybe I won't bother her with them ever again. It's not disgusting. It's just...what it is.*

He slipped one of his delicate hands inside the unbuttoned fly of his pajama pants, grasping the hard warmth that throbbed there.

He shut his eyes as he began to stroke, propping himself up with one hand against the toilet cistern as his breath began to quicken.

In his mind, Ella was in her white bikini, running after him down the beach. Her smile was alive, and her eyes were not empty. And that was enough to bring him to a rapid orgasm, tears prickling his eyeballs as he convulsed and spurted.

There. No mess. Straight into the toilet bowl. Neat and perfunctory, like the sad old fuck I am.

He flushed the toilet with an angry swipe of his hand and crept back to bed, his cheeks wet and his heart a cold rock in his chest.

* * *

87

The darkness screamed with triumph, and Ella thrilled at the sound.

"I'm coming, mummy. Are you ready? I'm coming."

"But the blood was dead."

"Yes, mummy, and so am I. But I'm coming anyway."

* * *

As Ella and Jonathon lay side by side in their bed, a thin runnel of milk began to drip from Ella's left breast, soaking through her nightshirt and pooling on the sheet beneath her.

The first cramp rippled through her belly, but it wasn't enough to wake her.

Not yet.

* * *

"There's something caught in this toilet."

Jonathon stared down into the bowl, his sleeves pushed up above his elbows, his brow furrowed. Ella paused. One half of her face was slathered in cold cream, the other was bare. She looked like a melting Phantom of the Opera.

"There is?" She forced herself to continue applying her face cream and ignore the slow churn of unease in her belly. She felt *guilty*, and wasn't sure why.

"Yeah. It won't flush properly. There must be something blocking the pipes."

"Well, we'd better call the plumber, then."

Jonathon blanched. His hand crept to his groin in an unconscious motion, and he shook his head.

"Oh…it will clear up by itself. These things usually do." He had no idea what he was talking about. Nor did he know why he thought his nighttime visit to the bathroom may have something to do with the blockage in the toilet. But he *did* think that, and he felt the overpowering urge to conceal his

(dirty – you're a dirty little boy, Johnny)

secret.

Ella nodded, too eagerly.

"Yes. We'll wait and see. I'm sure it's nothing."

She waited until Jonathon left the room before hunching over the sink, her hands gripping the porcelain rim, her face screwed up in pain.

"Ahhh," she breathed, "ohhh!"

What the hell is with these cramps? I don't have my period. I haven't had it in...

She blinked.

I haven't had a period in a little over nine months. That's a long time. I'm like clockwork. Why haven't I thought about this before now?

She looked at the red bag with the yellow moons, perched on the shelf on the bathroom wall. The fabric was coated with a thick layer of dust.

Haven't used it in a long time now.

She heard a rumbling from deep within the pipes in the wall, and turned around just in time to see an explosion of water gush up and out of the toilet bowl. She stumbled back, her tailbone connecting painfully with the edge of the sink, and shielded her face, gasping.

It was over as quickly as it began, and she looked around at the wet bathroom floor, her heart pounding. The pipes in the wall gave one more low groan and were silent.

My waters just broke, she thought, and smiled. It made no sense, but it was true. She knew it.

She glanced at the door to make sure Jonathon hadn't heard the blast of water and come running, and then she dropped to her knees, mopping up the water with a towel.

Her belly squeezed itself into another painful cramp as she mopped, and she sat on her haunches, grinning like a fool, until it passed.

She didn't bother looking into the toilet. She knew there was nothing there to see.

Yet.

* * *

"*I'm coming now, mummy. Come and get me. And mummy? I'm hungry.*"

"*Yes. Of course you are. Mummy will feed you. Come to mummy so mummy can love you and look after you and help you grow. I've waited so long for you, my sweetheart; so very long.*"

The darkness was so close now; so close.

It was time.

* * *

She shook Jonathon hard.

"Wake up! I need your help! We should both be there..."

"Whuh...?"

Jonathon rolled toward her, knuckling his eyes and squinting. She had turned on all the lights and he was dazzled.

"Get up," she said, smiling at him with more genuine pleasure than he'd seen on her face in all the years they'd been together. "We should both be there. I think *she* wants us both there. Yes, of course she would, it's only natural."

He was sitting up in bed now, staring at her.

"What *are* you talking about? Are you alright?"

"I'm fine, fine, brilliant, *perfect*, but it's time *now* and we need to go in there."

"In where, Ella?"

"In the bathroom, Jonathon. To the toilet."

For a suspended moment in time, he thought she knew about his release into the toilet all those months ago, and a terrified, shamefaced little boy reared up inside him, gibbering. He pushed it back down and shook his head, trying to find his footing in the strange new world he had awoken in.

"We need to go to the toilet right now?"

"That's *right*, come *on* Jonathon, she's *coming!*"

Jonathon had to lean over the edge of the bed to see her, because she dropped to all fours without warning and began whooping, her eyes squeezed shut.

"*Ohhh, ahh, ohhhOHHH...* "

She rocked back and forth in hypnotic movements, and he heard a loud bubbling splash in the bathroom as the toilet belched.

"Ella, *what the fuck is going on*? Are you alright? Do you need a doctor?"

She laughed, a thin reedy sound.

"No, I've never felt better. It's a normal process Jonathon. Women have been doing it for centuries. But we have to go in there *now* because she's coming no*oohhhw AHHH...*"

And she was gone, crawling to the bathroom.

He perched on the edge of the bed for a moment, gaping.

He saw her swaying hips, followed by her shuffling feet, disappear into the ensuite. She let out another one of those earsplitting howls and just beneath it, that splashing sound echoed in the bathroom again.

She really is *coming*, he thought without knowing he thought it, and he hit the floor running as he joined his wife in the bathroom.

Ella was kneeling before the toilet, a reverent worshipper paying her respects. She tilted her face up to Jonathon.

God, he thought, *she's radiant.*

She wrapped a warm hand around his wrist and pulled him down to the floor with her. She kissed him, her lips soft and hot. It was the first kiss they'd shared in over a year.

"Ready?" she said, and without waiting for his answer, she turned her face back to the toilet bowl. Watching with wide eyes. Waiting.

He stared at her, and as he did, she began to grunt, her abdomen heaving as she strained.

"Unnnghhh, hhh-UNGH, UUUNNNGGGHHH…"

The grunts came from a guttural place deep in her throat, and he felt the fine hairs all over his body stand on end. Blood was spilling down her thighs and spreading in a red fan across the tiles. She closed her eyes and seemed to drift, then the grunting and straining

(pushing – she's pushing)

began once more.

Jonathon didn't want to…but he turned his eyes toward the toilet bowl.

A shriveled walnut with a thick fuzz of black hair that waved to and fro in the water was emerging; sliding with painstaking slowness from the S-bend and into the toilet bowl.

Every time Ella stopped grunting and became silent, the thing in the toilet bowl slipped back out of sight. When Ella's noises and pushing began again, the thing in the bowl emerged a little bit more, making slow but steady progress.

Jonathon swallowed, then swallowed again. He seemed to have a huge brick in his throat and couldn't dislodge it. His heart fluttered so fast that he thought perhaps it had stopped, and his hands were balled into fists so tight that his fingernails sliced his palms.

"What the fuck is *tha-*"

"SHE'S COMING! SHE'S COMING!"

Ella's head whipped up, her hair flying wildly, and she lunged forward. Her hands gripped the toilet seat and she writhed, her hips swiveling, saliva dripping from her lower lip.

There was a *pop* from the toilet, and Ella screamed with ecstasy.

"*She's* crowned*! Her head is out and she's* beautiful, *oh Jonathon she's* beautiful, *look at her, look at her…*"

He took one step towards the toilet on autopilot, obeying Ella's urging. Then he stopped, panting with fear, confused.

"This can't be happening," he remarked to nobody, and nobody replied.

The walnut had become a baby's head, small and round and perfect, and as he stared in horror, the eyes opened. Hot black circles in the burning white of its

(her – it's a girl)

face. It blinked and watched him.

Ella gave a thunderous roar, and the pipes in the wall clanged and clattered.

Because little legs and feet are kicking inside them, trying to push themselves free, he thought, and felt his mind tilt a little on the axis of madness.

The head shot forward and became a head attached to shoulders, a torso, arms, and legs.

"She's here," Ella whispered, slumping back, exhausted. She lay curled in the small pool of blood, her hair trailing in it. "Our daughter is born. We've waited and wanted so long, and now she's here with us. She's beautiful, isn't she? Do you see her? Is she perfect?"

Jonathon was frozen with terror and revulsion. Not because it *was* a baby, but because it was a baby in their toilet, and it was crawling up and out. It was fast; and it was *growing*, right before his eyes.

Pulsing black veins throbbed and writhed beneath its translucent skin. As it clambered over the seat, Jonathon saw the umbilical cord that trailed out from its belly. It was a long rope of sopping wet toilet paper.

As Jonathon watched, the little being reached down and sliced with one hooked fingernail. The cord sluiced away from the thing's torso, severed, and a single pulse of black blood spurted. The paper cord sank into the bowl, and Jonathon was grateful that he couldn't see past the rim of the toilet from where he stood. He didn't want to see the placenta attached to that cord; no, not at all.

The baby-thing slithered over the edge of the toilet seat and hit the floor with a damp *shlump*.

"Ella," he breathed.

"Shhhh," she said. Her eyes were fixed on the thing worming its way toward her. She was still smiling. "Shhhh. Don't distract her. She's *hungry*."

The thing that couldn't be a baby but was, that couldn't be alive...and *wasn't*, wriggled over to the edge of the blood pool surrounding

(mummy)

Ella and stopped. It cast a glance over its chubby, oozing shoulder, smiled at Jonathon, and then dipped its head. A cracked black thing, roiling with growths

(that's its tongue! That's its tongue*! Oh fuck!)*

darted out from behind the cupid's bow of its lips, and began to lap at the blood like a kitten at a bowl of milk.

Jonathon fainted. He pitched forward and rebounded as his chest hit the side of the toilet. His unconscious body thudded down just behind the guzzling baby-thing and Ella hissed in annoyance.

"Be *careful* of her," she admonished Jonathon's immobile form, and the baby-thing gave a wet, gurgling giggle, still licking the blood from the floor.

"Don't you want a proper feed, little one?" Ella said, reaching out her hand. The creature lifted its head. It fixed the black saucers of its eyes on her, and opened its mouth. Triple rows of darning-needle teeth lined the black furrows of its gums. It was already at least five times the size it had been when it crawled out of the toilet.

"Come here, darling. My precious, my little one, my baby, my daughter. Come here, and let mummy feed you."

The thing was on her in a flash, and Ella's eyes rolled back in her head, her mouth lolling open.

Oh it hurts, and it's exquisite, and it's agony, and I love you, and you're mine, and nobody will ever take you away, and I'm so glad you're here, and oh that hurts...

But don't stop, baby. If it's what you need, don't stop.

Anything. Anything for you.

* * *

Ella named her L'il. The word took on a deeper gravity and meaning – a *power* – when she gifted her daughter with it, and she knew it was the right one.

Meg would approve...of some of it, anyway. Was it the cup she gave me that helped me conceive L'il? Was that what helped her grow in the womb of the pipes when my own womb couldn't hold her? I don't know. I think maybe that was part of it, but mostly I think it was my blood, my dead blood, and my wanting. And something Jonathon did, too. I don't know what that was, but I have an idea. I have a pretty good idea.

It didn't hurt *so* much anymore to feed her daughter; or maybe she was just used to it. The only real pain came when L'il latched on at the beginning of each feed; when she sank those hundreds of fangs, now as long and sharp as skewers, into the tender tissue around Ella's areola. L'il's teeth connected somewhere in the middle of Ella's inner breast, and when they were secured there, she began to drink.

Milk and blood flowed down the strange baby's gullet, and once the pain subsided to a dull throb, Ella treasured those moments. They were so close. They were joined.

She was a mother.

Lil's obsidian eyes closed, and her webbed fingers opened and shut against Ella's breast as she sated herself. Little moist snuffles came from the weeping nostrils set deep in her flat nose. Ella lovingly wiped away the trickles of blood that leaked from the corners of L'il's mouth while she fed.

"You're beautiful," she cooed to her baby, stroking the crawling slime of her skin, tracing the writhing black paths of her jumping veins.

L'il was starting to need more than just bloody milk. She had grown to the size of a four year old child already, and her body needed more sustenance than Ella's body alone could give.

That was alright. Ella had put Jonathon in the deep chest freezer last week, after L'il had torn out his throat. When the time came, he would nourish their daughter for at least a week or two. She was *his* daughter, too.

He'd fought at the end, and screamed, and said terrible things; but Ella knew he wanted to help their daughter. Or *would* have wanted to, if he'd been able to think straight.

And after there was no more daddy flesh? Then there was Pig the Pug, who would do for a few L'il meals. And then? Well, it didn't matter. Whatever it took, Ella would do it.

She would do anything.

What mother wouldn't?

Gardeners

David Dunwoody's first novel, Empire, was published in April 2008. Other publications include stories in all four volumes of Permuted Press' The Undead series, Abominations from Shroud Press, and Fried! from Graveside Tales Press. He is currently at work on the online serial The Harvest Cycle. A complete list of works and links to free fiction are available at daviddunwoody.com. Dave is currently (un)settled in Utah.

Allison M. Dickson was born in the tiny town of Oxford, OH in October, 1979. In second grade, her penchant for penning horror stories was discovered when, in a class assignment asking students who they'd like to be one day, she answered "Freddy Krueger." At eleven years of age, she discovered the works of Stephen King, and the beautiful world of the macabre opened up before her. In the nearly twenty years since, her dream of becoming a writer rarely wavered. The realm of blogging became a her main outlet in 2005, and when she's not penning fiction, she can still be found expounding on topics ranging between pop culture, film, politics, and parenting, all peppered with her signature caustic wit. Robert Heinlein, George Orwell, and Richard Matheson are among her other literary inspirations, but she draws most of her wisdom from her closest friends, colleagues, and her very vivid dreams. Allison currently resides and attends college in the beautiful Pacific Northwest with her husband Ken and her two children, Natalie and Elias.

Gardeners

Felicity Dowker is an emerging author of speculative fiction. She lives in Victoria, Australia, with her partner and their two young children. Felicity is an active member of the Australian Horror Writers Association, and has had her work accepted for publication in a variety of magazines and anthologies, including Andromeda Spaceways Inflight Magazine, Borderlands, Midnight Echo, Antipodean SF, and others. Her first published piece, "Windows to the Soul", was recently nominated for an Aurealis Award, and she will soon begin reviewing for The Specusphere. In between penning weird tales, enjoying her family, and working at her day job, Felicity drinks far too much coffee and maintains a blog at http://www.holeinthepage.blogspot.com. But enter, stranger, at your riske: here there be Tygers.

Sharon M. White lives in Erwin, Tennessee with her husband and their children. She uses her writing as a way to explore the dark side of life and the unknown and then she presents her findings to you, the reader. Horror is her main genre but she also writes poetry and dark fantasies. Her works have appeared in several magazines, both online and in print, such as Enigma, Bewildering Stories, Whispers of Wickedness, Down in the Dirt, and many more. Works by Sharon will be featured in the upcoming Northern Haunts anthology from Shroud Publishing and a future issue of Doorways Magazine.

Gardeners

 **Jodi Lee** is a writer and editor from Manitoba, Canada. She has spent her entire life on the Canadian Prairies, which she credits for her over-active imagination. She has decided that nothing breaks the monotony like the occasional zombie or flesh-devouring mutant alien mosquito chasing her two daughters. She's often found slicing and dicing prose in her positions as Editor in Chief of LBF Books, Senior Editor at Lachesis Publishing and Submissions/Copy Editor at Apex Book Company.

Her fiction has appeared Night to Dawn and Nocturnal Ooze as well as the anthologies Echoes of Terror (Lachesis Publishing), Fried! Fast Food, Slow Deaths (Graveside Tales), Parasitic Thoughts (The Parasitorium Group) and the upcoming Tainted (Strange Publications) and The Black Garden (Corpulent Insanity). She is credited as co-author for the opening and closing pieces in her first horror anthology editing credit: Courting Morpheus.

 **Aaron Polson** is a high school English teacher who dreams in black and white while Rod Serling narrates. When he isn't arguing about the definition of irony with his students, he can be found chipping away at some twisted tale. He currently resides in Lawrence, Kansas with his wife, two sons, and a tattooed rabbit. His short fiction has appeared in Reflection's Edge, Necrotic Tissue, Permuted Press's Monstrous anthology, and other publications. You can visit him on the web at www.aaronpolson.com.

Gardeners

Evan J. Peterson's work has recently been featured in the Southeast Review, The Pinch, and CaKe, and online at LaFovea.org and Qarrtsiluni.com. He is currently composing a poetry manuscript that focuses on monstrosity, film, and identity.

Sam W. Anderson was born a poor, black child. After leaving home to find his "special purpose," he found work at a service station, as a cat juggler and as a carnival barker while achieving his life-long dream of appearing in the phone book. Later, he invented the opti-grab, earning a fortune before losing it to a class-action law suit. Along the way, he tapped Bernadette Peters.

Oh, wait…that's Navin R. Johnson.

Sam W. Anderson lives in Denver, Colorado with his wife, two children, two dogs and several skeletons taking up residence in his closet. His fiction has appeared in many venues: online, print magazines and anthologies. POSTCARDS FROM PURGATORY, a collection of his early short stories will be available from Doorways Publishing late summer, 2008.

Gardeners

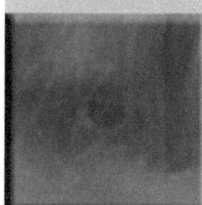 **Christopher Allan Death** currently resides in the concrete jungle of Northern Colorado. He has published fiction in Worlds of Wonder, Night to Dawn, 7th Dimension Magazine, Bits of the Dead (Coscom Entertainment), and Deadlines (Comet Press), among others.

His novella, WELCOME TO WONDERLAND, is now available from Lyrical Press, Inc. You can find him at www.myspace.com/christopherdeath.

www.ingramcontent.com/pod-product-compliance
Lightning Source LLC
Chambersburg PA
CBHW031852170626
46807CB00004B/1694